THE TOR DOUBLES

Tor is proud to bring you the best in science fiction's short novels. An amazing amount of particularly fine science fiction is written at a length just too short to put in a book by itself, so we're providing them two at a time.

The Tor Doubles will be both new stories and older ones, all carefully chosen. Whichever side you start with, you will be able to turn the book over and enjoy the other side just as much.

SHE WOULD BE A WOMAN.
IF SHE RETURNED.

The tempers come, moans tiding in, then the battle data. As it passed into her subconscious, she caught a flash of—

Rocks and ice, a thick cloud of dust and gas glowing red but seeming dark, no stars no constellation guides this time. The beacon came on. That would be her only way to orient once the gloves stopped inertial and locked onto the target.

The seedship
was like
a shadow within a shadow
twenty-two kilometers across, yet
carrying
only six
teams
LAUNCH *she flies!*

GREG BEAR

HARDFOUGHT

A TOM DOHERTY ASSOCIATES BOOK
NEW YORK

Reprinted by permission of the author and his agent, Richard Curtis
Associates, Inc.

HARDFOUGHT

A TOR Book
Published by Tom Doherty Associates, Inc.
49 West 24 Street
New York, NY 10010

Cover art by Tony Roberts

ISBN: 0-812-55971-1   Can. ISBN: 0-812-55951-7

First edition: November 1988

Printed in the United States of America

0 9 8 7 6 5 4 3 2 1

In the Han Dynasty, historians were appointed by the royal edict to write the history of Imperial China. They alone were the arbiters of what would be recorded. Although various emperors tried, none could gain access to the ironbound chest in which each document was placed after it was written. The historians preferred to suffer death rather than betray their trust.

At the end of each reign the box would be opened and the documents published, perhaps to benefit the next emperor. But for these documents, Imperial China, to a large extent, has no history.

The thread survives by whim.

Humans called it the Medusa. Its long twisted ribbons of gas strayed across fifty parsecs, glowing blue, yellow, and carmine. Its central core was a ghoulish green flecked with watery black. Half a dozen protostars circled the core, and as many more dim conglomerates pooled in dimples in the nebula's magnetic field. The Medusa was a huge womb of stars—and disputed territory.

Whenever Prufrax looked at it in displays or through the ship's ports, it seemed malevolent, like a zealous mother showing an ominous face to protect her children. Prufrax had never had a mother, but she had seen them in some of the fibs.

At five, Prufrax was old enough to know the *Mellangee's* mission and her role in it. She had already been through four ship-years of indoctrination. Until her first battle she would be educated in both the Know and the Tell. She would be exercised and trained in the Mocks; in sleep she would dream of penetrating the huge red-and-white Senexi seedships and finding the brood mind. "Zap, Zap," she went with her lips, silent so the tellman wouldn't think her thoughts were straying.

The tellman peered at her from his position in the center of the spherical classroom. Her mates stared straight at the center, all focusing somewhere around the tellman's spiderlike teaching desk, waiting for the trouble, some fidgeting. "How many branch individuals in the Senexi brood mind?" he asked. He looked around the classroom. Peered face by face. Focused on her again. "Pru?"

"Five," she said. Her arms ached. She had been pumped full of moans the wake before. She was already three meters tall, in elfstate, with her long, thin limbs not nearly adequately fleshed out and her fingers still crisscrossed with the surgery done to adapt them to the gloves.

"What will you find in the brood mind?" the tellman pursued, his impassive face stretched across a hammerhead as wide as his shoulders. Some of the fems thought tellmen were attractive. Not many—and Pru was not one of them.

"Yoke," she said.

"What is in the brood-mind yoke?"

"Fibs."

"More specifically? And it really isn't all fib, you know."

"Info. Senexi data."

"What will you do?"

"Zap," she said, smiling.

"Why, Pru?"

"Yoke has team gens-memory. Zap yoke, spill the life of the team's five branch inds."

"Zap the brood, Pru?"

"No," she said solemnly. That was a new instruction, only in effect since her class's inception. "Hold the brood for the supreme overs." The tellman did not say what would be done with the Senexi broods. That was not her concern.

"Fine," said the tellman. "You tell well, for someone who's always half-journeying."

Brainwalk, Prufrax thought. Tellman was fancy with the words, but to Pru, what she was prone to do during Tell was brainwalk, seeking out her future. She was already five, soon six. Old. Some saw Senexi by the time they were four.

"Zap, Zap," she went with her lips.

Aryz skidded through the thin layer of liquid ammonia on his broadest pod, considering his new assignment. He knew the Medusa by another name, one that conveyed all the time and effort the Senexi had invested in it. The protostar nebula held few mysteries for him. He and his four branch-mates, who along with the all-important brood mind comprised

one of the six teams aboard the seedship, had patrolled
the nebula for ninety-three orbits, each orbit—including the timeless periods outside status geometry—
taking some one hundred and thirty human years.
They had woven in and out of the tendrils of gas,
charting the infalling masses and exploring the rocky
accretion disks of stars entering the main sequence.
With each measure and update, the brood minds
refined their view of the nebula as it would be a
hundred generations hence, when the Senexi plan
would finally mature.

The Senexi were nearly as old as the galaxy. They
had achieved spaceflight during the time of the star-
globe, when the galaxy had been a sphere. They had
not been a quick or brilliant race. Each great achieve-
ment had taken thousands of generations, and not just
because of their material handicaps. In those times,
elements heavier than helium had been rare, found
only around stars that had greedily absorbed huge
amounts of primeval hydrogen, burned fierce and blue
and exploded early, permeating the ill-defined galactic
arms with carbon and nitrogen, lithium and oxygen.
Elements heavier than iron had been almost non-
existent. The biologies of cold gas-giant worlds had
developed with a much smaller palette of chemical
combinations in producing the offspring of the pri-
mary Population II stars.

Aryz, even with the limited perspective of a branch
ind, was aware that, on the whole, the humans
opposing the seedship were more adaptable, more
vital. But they were not more experienced. The Senexi
with their billions of years had often matched them.

And Aryz's perspective was expanding with each day of his new assignment.

In the early generations of the struggle, Senexi mental stasis and cultural inflexibility had made them avoid contact with the Population I species. They had never begun a program of extermination of the younger, newly life-forming worlds; the task would have been monumental and probably useless. So when spacefaring cultures developed, the Senexi had retreated, falling back into the redoubts of old stars even before engaging with the new kinds. They had retreated for three generations, about thirty thousand human years, raising their broods on cold nestworlds around red dwarfs, conserving, holding back for the inevitable conflicts.

As the Senexi had anticipated, the younger Population I races had found need of even the aging groves of the galaxy's first stars. They had moved in savagely, voraciously, with all the strength and mutability of organisms evolved from a richer soup of elements. Biology had, in some ways, evolved in its own right and superseded the Senexi.

Aryz raised the upper globe of his body, with its five silicate eyes arranged in a cross along the forward surface. He had memory of those times, and times long before, though his team hadn't existed then. The brood mind carried memories selected from the total store of nearly twelve billion years' experience; an awesome amount of knowledge, even to a Senexi. He pushed himself forward with his rear pods.

Through the brood mind Aryz could share the memories of a hundred thousand past generations, yet

the brood mind itself was younger than its branch of
individuals. For a time in their youth, in their liquid-
dwelling larval form, the branch inds carried their own
sacs of data, each a fragment of the total necessary for
complete memory. The branch inds swam through
ammonia seas and wafted through thick warm gaseous
zones, protoplasmic blobs three to four meters in
diameter—developing their personalities under the
weight of the past—and not even a complete past. No
wonder they were inflexible, Aryz thought. Most
branch inds were aware enough to see that—especially
when they were allowed to compare histories with the
Population I species, as he was doing—but there was
nothing to be done. They were content the way they
were. To change would be unspeakably repugnant.
Extinction was preferable . . . almost.

But now they were pressed hard. The brood mind
had begun a number of experiments. Aryz's team had
been selected from the seedship's contingent to over-
see the experiments, and Aryz had been chosen as the
chief investigator. Two orbits past, they had captured
six human embryos in a breeding device, as well as a
highly coveted memory storage center. Most Senexi
engagements had been with humans for the past three
or four generations. Just as the Senexi dominated
Population II species, humans were ascendant among
their kind.

Experiments with the human embryos had already
been conducted. Some had been allowed to develop
normally; others had been tampered with, for reasons
Aryz was not aware of. The tamperings had not been
very successful.

The newer experiments, Aryz suspected, were going to take a different direction, and the seedship's actions now focused on him; he believed he would be given complete authority over the human shapes. Most branch inds would have dissipated under such a burden, but not Aryz. He found the human shapes rather interesting, in their own horrible way. They might, after all, be the key to Senexi survival.

The moans were toughening her elfstate. She lay in pain for a wake, not daring to close her eyes; her mind was changing and she feared sleep would be the end of her. Her nightmares were not easily separated from life; some, in fact, were sharper.

Too often in sleep she found herself in a Senexi trap, struggling uselessly, being pulled in deeper, her hatred wasted against such power. . . .

When she came out of the rigor, Prufrax was given leave by the subordinate tellman. She took to the *Mellangee's* greenroads, walking stiffly in the shallow gravity. Her hands itched. Her mind seemed almost empty after the turmoil of the past few wakes. She had never felt so calm and clear. She hated the Senexi double now; once for their innate evil, twice for what they had made her overs put her through to be able to fight them. Logic did not matter. She was calm, assured. She was growing more mature wake by wake. Fight-budding, the tellman called it, hate coming out like blooms, synthesizing the sunlight of his teaching into pure fight.

The greenroads rose temporarily beyond the labyrinth shields and armor of the ship. Simple transparent

plastic and steel geodesic surfaces formed a lacework
over the gardens, admitting radiation necessary to the
vegetation growing along the paths. No machines
scooted one forth and inboard here. It was necessary to
walk. Walking was luxury and privilege.

Prufrax looked down on the greens to each side of
the paths without much comprehension. They were
beautiful. Yes, one should say that, but what did it
mean? Pleasing? She wasn't sure what being pleased
meant, outside of thinking Zap. She sniffed a flower
that, the signs explained, bloomed only in the light of
young stars not yet fusing. They were near such a star
now, and the greenroads were shiny black and electric
green with the blossoms. Lamps had been set out for
other plants unsuited to such darkened conditions.
Some technic allowed suns to appear in selected
plastic panels when viewed from certain angles.
Clever, the technicals.

She much preferred the looks of a technical to a
tellman, but she was common in that. Technicals
required brainflex, tellmen cargo capacity. Technicals
were strong and ran strong machines, like in the
adventure fibs, where technicals were often the pro-
tags. She wished a technical were on the greenroads
with her. The moans had the effect of making her
receptive—what she saw, looking in mirrors, was a
certain shine in her eyes—but there was no chance of
a breeding liaison. She was quite unreproductive in
this moment of elfstate. Other kinds of meetings were
not unusual.

She looked up and saw a figure at least a hundred
meters away, sitting on an allowed patch near the path.

She walked casually, as gracefully as possible with the stiffness. Not a technical, she saw soon, but she was not disappointed. Too calm.

"Over," he said as she approached.

"Under," she replied. But not by much—he was probably six or seven ship years old and not easily classifiable.

"Such a fine elfstate," he commented. His hair was black. He was shorter than she, but something in his build reminded her of the glovers. She accepted his compliment with a nod and pointed to a spot near him. He motioned for her to sit, and she did so with a whuff, massaging her knees.

"Moans?" he asked.

"Bad stretch," she said.

"You're a glover." He was looking at the fading scars on her hands.

"Can't tell what you are," she said.

"Noncombat," he said. "Tuner of the mandates."

She knew very little about the mandates, except that law decreed every ship carry one, and few of the crew were ever allowed to peep. "Noncombat, hm?" she mused. She didn't despise him for that; one never felt strong negatives for a crew member. She didn't feel much of anything. Too calm.

"Been working on ours this wake," he said. "Too hard, I guess. Told to walk." Overzealousness in work was considered an erotic trait aboard the *Mellangee*. Still, she didn't feel too receptive toward him.

"Glovers walk after a rough growing," she said.

He nodded. "My name's Clevo."

"Prufrax."

"Combat soon?"

"Hoping. Waiting forever."

"I know. Just been allowed access to the mandate for a half-dozen wakes. All new to me. Very happy."

"Can you talk about it?" she asked. Information about the ship not accessible in certain rates was excellent barter.

"Not sure," he said, frowning. "I've been told caution."

"Well, I'm listening."

He could come from glover stock, she thought, but probably not from technical. He wasn't very muscular, but he wasn't as tall as a glover, or as thin, either.

"If you'll tell me about gloves."

With a smile she held up her hands and wriggled the short, stumpy fingers. "Sure."

The brood mind floated weightless in its tank, held in place by buffered carbon rods. Metal was at a premium aboard the Senexi ships, more out of tradition than actual material limitations. From what Aryz could tell, the Senexi used metals sparingly for the same reason—and he strained to recall the small dribbles of information about the human past he had extracted from the memory store—for the same reason **that the Romans of old Earth regarded farming as the only truly noble occupation**—

Farming being the raising of *plants* for food and raw materials. *Plants* were analogous to the freeth Senexi ate in their larval youth, but the freeth were not green and sedentary.

There was almost a certain fascination in stretching

his mind to encompass human concepts. He had had so little time to delve deeply—and that was good, of course, for he had been set to answer specific questions, not mire himself in the whole range of human filth.

He floated before the brood mind, all these thoughts coursing through his tissues. He had no central nervous system, no truly differentiated organs except those that dealt with the outside world—limbs, eyes, permea. The brood mind, however, was all central nervous system, a thinly buffered sac of viscous fluids about ten meters wide.

"Have you investigated the human memory device yet?" the brood mind asked.

"I have."

"Is communication with the human shapes possible for us?"

"We have already created interfaces for dealing with their machines. Yes, it seems likely we can communicate."

"Does it occur to you that in our long war with humans, we have made no attempt to communicate before?"

This was a complicated question. It called for several qualities that Aryz, as a branch ind, wasn't supposed to have. Inquisitiveness, for one. Branch inds did not ask questions. They exhibited initiative only as offshoots of the brood mind.

He found, much to his dismay, that the question had occurred to him. "We have never captured a human memory store before," he said, by way of incomplete answer. "We could not have communicated without such an extensive source of information."

"Yet, as you say, even in the past we have been able to use human machines."

"The problem is vastly more complex."

The brood mind paused. "Do you think the teams have been prohibited from communicating with humans?"

Aryz felt the closest thing to anguish possible for a branch ind. Was he being considered unworthy? Accused of conduct inappropriate to a branch ind? His loyalty to the brood mind was unshakable. "Yes."

"And what might our reasons be?"

"Avoidance of pollution."

"Correct. We can no more communicate with them and remain untainted than we can walk on their worlds, breathe their atmosphere." Again, silence. Aryz lapsed into a mode of inactivity. When the brood mind readdressed him, he was instantly aware.

"Do you know how you are different?" it asked.

"I am not . . ." Again, hesitation. Lying to the brood mind was impossible for him. What snared him was semantics, a complication in the radiated signals between them. He had not been aware that he was different; the brood mind's questions suggested he might be. But he could not possibly face up to the fact and analyze it all in one short time. He signaled his distress.

"You are useful to the team," the brood mind said. Aryz calmed instantly. His thoughts became sluggish, receptive. There was a possibility of redemption. But how was he different? "You are to attempt communication with the shapes yourself. You will not engage in any discourse with your fellows while you are so involved." He was banned. "And after completion of this mission and transfer of certain facts to me, you will dissipate."

Aryz struggled with the complexity of the orders. "How am I different, worthy of such a commission?"

The surface of the brood mind was as still as an undisturbed pool. The indistinct black smudges that marked its radiative organs circulated slowly within the interior, then returned, one above the other, to focus on him. "You will grow a new branch ind. It will not have your flaws, but, then again, it will not be useful to me should such a situation come a second time. Your dissipation will be a relief, but it will be regretted."

"How am I different?"

"I think you know already," the brood mind said. "When the time comes, you will feed the new branch ind all your memories but those of human contact. If you do not survive to that stage of its growth, you will pick your fellow who will perform that function for you."

A small pinkish spot appeared on the back of Aryz's globe. He floated forward and placed his largest permeum against the brood mind's cool surface. The key and command were passed, and his body became capable of reproduction. Then the signal of dismissal was given. He left the chamber.

Flowing through the thin stream of liquid ammonia lining the corridor, he felt ambiguously stimulated. His was a position of privilege and anathema. He had been blessed—and condemned. Had any other branch ind experienced such a thing?

Then he knew the brood mind was correct. He was different from his fellows. None of them would have asked such questions. None of them could have survived the suggestion of communicating with human shapes. If this task hadn't been given to him, he would have had to dissipate away.

The pink spot grew larger, then began to make greyish flakes. It broke through the skin, and casually, almost without thinking, Aryz scraped it off against a bulkhead. It clung, made a radio-frequency emanation something like a sigh, and began absorbing nutrients from the ammonia.

Aryz went to inspect the shapes.

She was intrigued by Clevo, but the kind of interest she felt was new to her. She was not particularly receptive. Rather, she felt a mental gnawing as if she were hungry, or had been injected with some kind of brain moans. What Clevo told her about the mandates opened up a topic she had never considered before. How did all things come to be—and how did she figure in them?

The mandates were quite small, Clevo explained, each little more than a cubic meter in volume. Within them was the entire history and culture of the human species, as accurate as possible, culled from all existing sources. The mandate in each ship was updated whenever the ship returned to a contact station. It was not likely the *Mellangee* would return to a contact station during their lifetimes, with the crew leading such short lives on the average.

Clevo had been assigned small tasks—checking

data and adding ship records—that had allowed him to sample bits of the mandate. "It's mandated that we have records," he explained, "and what we have, you see, is *man-data*." He smiled. "That's a joke," he said. "Sort of."

Prufrax nodded solemnly. "So where do we come from?"

"Earth, of course," Clevo said. "Everyone knows that."

"I mean, where do we come from—you and I, the crew."

"Breeding division. Why ask? You know."

"Yes." She frowned, concentrating. "I mean, we don't come from the same place as the Senexi. The same way."

"No, that's foolishness."

She saw that it was foolishness—the Senexi were different all around. What was she struggling to ask? "Is their fib like our own?"

"Fib? History's not a fib. Not most of it, anyway. Fibs are for unreal. History is overfib."

She knew, in a vague way, that fibs were unreal. She didn't like to have their comfort demeaned, though. "Fibs are fun," she said. "They teach Zap."

"I suppose," Clevo said dubiously. "Being non-combat, I don't see Zap fibs."

Fibs without Zap were almost unthinkable to her. "Such dull," she said.

"Well, of course you'd say that. I might find Zap fibs dull—think of that?"

"We're different," she said. "Like Senexi are different."

Clevo's jaw hung over. "No way. We're crew. We're human. Senexi are . . ." He shook his head as if fed bitters.

"No, I mean . . ." She paused, uncertain whether she was entering unallowed territory. "You and I, we're fed different, given different moans. But in a big way we're different from Senexi. They aren't made, nor act, as you and I. But . . ." Again it was difficult to express. She was irritated. "I don't want to talk to you anymore."

A tellman walked down the path, not familiar to Prufrax. He held out his hand for Clevo, and Clevo grasped it. "It's amazing," the tellman said, "how you two gravitate to each other. Go, elfstate, he addressed Prufrax. "You're on the wrong greenroad."

She never saw the young researcher again. With glover training underway, the itches he aroused soon faded, and Zap resumed its overplace.

The Senexi had ways of knowing humans were near. As information came in about fleets and individual cruisers less than one percent nebula diameter distant, the seedship seemed warmer, less hospitable. Everything was UV with anxiety, and the new branch ind on the wall had to be shielded by a special silicate cup to prevent distortion. The brood mind grew a corniculum automatically, though the toughened outer membrane would be of little help if the seedship was breached.

Aryz had buried his personal confusion under a load of work. He had penetrated the human memory store deeply enough to find instruction on its use. It called itself a *mandate* (the human word came through the interface as a correlated series of radiated symbols), and even the simple preliminary directions were difficult for Aryz. It was like swimming in another family's private sea, though of course infinitely more alien; how could he connect with experiences never had, problems and needs never encountered by his kind?

He could speak some of the human languages in several radio frequencies, but he hadn't yet decided how he was going to produce modulated sounds for the human shapes. It was a disturbing prospect. What would he vibrate? A permeum could vibrate subtly—such signals were used when branch inds joined to form the brood mind—but he doubted his control would ever be subtle enough. Sooner expect a human to communicate with a Senexi by controlling the radiations of its nervous system! The humans had distinct organs within their breathing passages that produced the vibrations; perhaps those structures could be mimicked. But he hadn't yet studied the dead shapes in much detail.

He observed the new branch ind once or twice each watch period. Never before had he seen an induced replacement. The normal process was for two brood minds to exchange plasm and form new team buds, then to exchange and nurture the buds. The buds were later cast free to swim as individual larvae. While the larvae often swam through the liquid and gas atmosphere of a Senexi world for thousands, even tens of thousands of kilometers, inevitably they returned to gather with the other buds of their team. Replacements were selected from a separately created pool of "generic" buds only if one or more originals had been destroyed during their wanderings. The destruction of a complete team meant reproductive failure.

In a mature team, only when a branch ind was destroyed did the brood mind induce a replacement. In essence, then, Aryz was already considered dead.

Yet he was still useful. That amused him, if the Senexi emotion could be called amusement. Restricting himself from his fellows was difficult, but he filled the time by immersing himself, through the interface, in the mandate.

The humans were also connected with the mandate through their surrogate parent, and in this manner they were quiescent.

He reported infrequently to the brood mind. Until he had established communication, there was little to report.

And throughout his turmoil, like the others he could sense a fight was coming. It could determine the success or failure of all their work in the nebula. In the grand scheme, failure here might not be crucial. But the Senexi had taken the long view too often in the past. Their age and experience—their calmness— were working against them. How else to explain the decision to communicate with human shapes? Where would such efforts lead? If he succeeded.

And he knew himself well enough to doubt he would fail.

He could feel an affinity for them already, peering at them through the thick glass wall in their isolated chamber, his skin paling at the thought of their heat, their poisonous chemistry. A diseased affinity. He hated himself for it. And reveled in it. It was what made him particularly useful to the team. If he was defective, and this was the only way he could serve, then so be it.

The other branch inds observed his passings from a distance, making no judgments. Aryz was dead, though he worked and moved. His sacrifice had been fearful. Yet he would not be a hero. His kind could never be emulated.

It was a horrible time, a horrible conflict.

She floated in language, learned it in a trice; there were no distractions. She floated in history and picked up as much as she could, for the source seemed inexhaustible. She tried to distinguish between eyes-open—the barren, pale grey-brown chamber with the thick green wall, beyond which floated a murky roundness—and eyes-shut, when she dropped back into language and history with no fixed foundation.

Eyes-open, she saw the Mam with its comforting limbs and its soft voice, its tubes and extrusions of food and its hissings and removal of waste. Through Mam's wires she learned. Mam also tended another like herself, and another, and one more unlike any of them, more like the shape beyond the green wall.

She was very young, and it was all a mystery.

At least she knew her name. And what she was supposed to do. She took small comfort in that.

They fitted Prufrax with her gloves, and she went into the practice chamber, dragged by her gloves almost, for she hadn't yet knitted her plug-in nerves in the right index digit and her pace control was uncertain.

There, for six wakes straight, she flew with the other glovers back and forth across the dark spaces like elfstate comets. Constellations and nebula aspects flashed at random on the distant walls, and she oriented to them like a night-flying bird. Her glovemates were Ornin, an especially slender male, and Ban, a red-haired female, and the special-projects sisters, Ya, Trice, and Damu, new from the breeding division.

When she let the gloves have their way, she was freer than she had ever felt before. Did the gloves really control? The question wasn't important. Control was somewhere uncentered, behind her eyes and beyond her fingers, as if she were drawn on a beautiful silver wire where it was best to go. Doing what was best to do. She barely saw the field that flowed from the grip of the thick, solid gloves or felt its caressing, life-sustaining influence. Truly, she hardly saw or felt anything but situations, targets, opportunities, the success or failure of the Zap. Failure was an acute pain. She was never reprimanded for failure; the reprimand was in her blood, and she felt as if she wanted to die. But then the opportunity would improve, the Zap would succeed, and everything around her—stars, Senexi seedship, the *Mellangee*, everything—seemed part of a beautiful dream all her own.

She was intense in the Mocks.

Their initial practice over, the entry play began.

One by one, the special-projects sisters took their

hyperbolic formation. Their glove fields threw out extensions, and they combined force. In they went, the mock Senexi seedship brilliant red and white and UV and radio and hateful before them. Their tails swept through the seedship's outer shields and swirled like long silk hair laid on water; they absorbed fantastic energies, grew brighter like violent little stars against the seedship outline. They were engaged in the drawing of the shields, and sure as topology, the spirals of force had to have a dimple on the opposite side that would iris wide enough to let in glovers. The sisters twisted the forces, and Prufrax could see the dimple stretching out under them—

The exercise ended. The elfstate glovers were cast into sudden dark. Prufrax came out of the mock unprepared, her mind still bent on the Zap. The lack of orientation drove her as mad as a moth suddenly flipped from night to day. She careened until gently mitted and channeled. She flowed down a tube, the field slowly neutralizing, and came to a halt still gloved, her body jerking and tingling.

"What the breed happened?" she screamed, her hands beginning to hurt.

"Energy conserve," a mechanical voice answered. Behind Prufrax, the other elfstate glovers lined up in the catch tube, all but the special-projects sisters. Ya, Trice, and Damu had been taken out of the exercise early and replaced by simulations. There was no way their functions could be mocked. They entered the tube ungloved and helped their comrades adjust to the overness of the real.

As they left the mock chamber, another batch of

glovers, even younger and fresher in elfstate, passed them. Ya held her hands up, and they saluted in return. "Breed more every day," Prufrax grumbled. She worried about having so many crew she'd never be able to conduct a satisfactory Zap herself. Where would the honor of being a glover go if everyone was a glover?

She wriggled into her cramped bunk, feeling exhilarated and irritated. She replayed the mocks and added in the missing Zap, then stared gloomily at her small, narrow feet.

Out there the Senexi waited. Perhaps they were in the same state as she—ready to fight, testy at being reined in. She pondered her ignorance, her inability to judge whether such things were even possible among the enemy. She thought of the researcher, Clevo. "Blank," she murmured. "Blank, blank." Such thoughts were unnecessary, and humanizing Senexi was unworthy of a glover.

Aryz looked at the instrument, stretched a pod into it, and willed. Vocal human language came out the other end, thin and squeaky in the helium atmosphere. The sound disgusted and thrilled him. He removed the instrument from the gelatinous strands of the engineering wall and pushed it into his interior through a stretched permeum. He took a thick draft of ammonia and slid to the human shapes chamber again.

He pushed through the narrow port into the observation room. Adjusting his eyes to the heat and bright light beyond the transparent wall, he saw the round mututed shape first—the result of their unsuccessful experiments. He swung his sphere around and looked at the others.

For a time he couldn't decide which was uglier—the mutated shape or the normals. Then he thought of what it would be like to have humans tamper with Senexi and try to make them into human forms. . . . He looked at the round human and shrunk as if from sudden heat. Aryz had had nothing to do with the experiments. For that, at least, he was grateful.

Apparently, even before fertilization, human buds—eggs—were adapted for specific roles. The healthy human shapes appeared sufficiently different—discounting *sexual* characteristics—to indicate some variation in function. They were four-podded, two-opticked, with auditory apparatus and olfactory organs mounted on the *head*, along with one permeum, the *mouth*. At least, he thought, they were hairless, unlike some of the other Population I species Aryz had learned about in the mandate.

Aryz placed the tip of the vocalizer against a sound-transmitting plate and spoke.

"Zello," came the sound within the chamber. The mutated shape looked up. It lay on the floor, great bloated stomach backed by four almost useless pods. It usually made high-pitched sounds continuously. Now it stopped and listened, straining on the tube that connected it to the breed-supervising device.

"Hello," replied the male. It sat on a ledge across the chamber, having unhooked itself.

The machine that served as surrogate parent and instructor stood in one corner, an awkward parody of a human, with limbs too long and head too small. Aryz could see the unwillingness of the designing engineers to examine human anatomy too closely.

"I am called—" Aryz said, his name emerging as a meaningless stretch of white noise. He would have to do better than that. He compressed and adapted the frequencies. "I am called Aryz."

"Hello," the young female said.

"What are your names?" He knew that well enough, having listened many times to their conversations.

"Prufrax," the female said. "I'm a glover."

The human shapes contained very little genetic memory. As a kind of brood marker, Aryz supposed, they had been equipped with their name, occupation, and the rudiments of environmental knowledge. This seemed to have been artificially imposed; in their natural state, very likely, they were born almost blank. He could not, however, be certain, since human reproductive chemistry was extraordinarily subtle and complicated.

"I'm a teacher, Prufrax," Aryz said. The logic structure of the language continued to be painful to him.

"I don't understand you," the female replied.

"You teach me, I teach you."

"We have the Mam," the male said, pointing to the machine. "She teaches us." The Mam, as they called it, was hooked into the mandate. Withholding that from the humans—the only equivalent, in essence, to the Senexi sac of memory—would have been unthinkable. It was bad enough that humans didn't come naturally equipped with their own share of knowledge.

"Do you know where you are?" Aryz asked.

"Where we live," Prufrax said. "Eyes-open."

Aryz opened a port to show them the stars and a portion of the nebula. "Can you tell me where you are by looking out the window?"

"Among the lights," Prufrax said.

Humans, then, did not instinctively know their positions by star patterns as other Population I species did.

"Don't talk to it," the male said. "Mam talks to us." Aryz consulted the mandate for some understanding of the name they had given to the breed-supervising machine. Mam, it explained, was probably a natural expression for womb-carrying parent. Aryz severed the machine's power.

"Mam is no longer functional," he said. He would have the engineering wall put together another less identifiable machine to link them to the mandate and to their nutrition. He wanted them to associate comfort and completeness with nothing but himself.

The machine slumped, and the female shape pulled herself free of the hookup. She started to cry, a reaction quite mysterious to Aryz. His link with the mandate had not been intimate enough to answer questions about the wailing and moisture from the eyes. After a time the male and female lay down and became dormant.

The mutated shape made more soft sounds and tried to approach the transparent wall. It held up its thin arms as if beseeching. The others would have nothing to do with it; now it wished to go with him. Perhaps the biologists had partially succeeded in their attempt at transformation; perhaps it was more Senexi than human.

Aryz quickly backed out through the port, into the cool and security of the corridor beyond.

It was an endless orbital dance, this detection and matching of course, moving away and swinging back, deceiving and revealing, between the *Mellangee* and the Senexi seedship. It was inevitable that the human ship should close in; human ships were faster, knew better the higher geometries.

Filled with her skill and knowledge, Prufrax waited, feeling like a ripe fruit about to fall from the tree. At this point in their training, just before the application, elfstates were very receptive. She was allowed to take a lover, and they were assigned small separate quarters near the outer greenroads.

The contact was satisfactory, as far as it went. Her mate was an older glover named Kumnax, and as they lay back in the cubicle, soothed by air-dance fibs, he told her stories about past battles, special tactics, how to survive.

"Survive?" she asked, puzzled.

"Of course." His long brown face was intent on the view of the greenroads through the cubicle's small window.

"I don't understand," she said.

"Most glovers don't make it," he said patiently.

"I will."

He turned to her. "You're six," he said. "You're very young. I'm ten. I've seen. You're about to be applied for the first time, you're full of confidence.

But most glovers won't make it. They breed thousands of us. We're expendable. We're based on the best glovers of the past, but even the best don't survive."

"I will," Prufrax repeated, her jaw set.

"You always say that," he murmured.

Prufrax stared at him for a moment.

"Last time I knew you," he said, "you kept saying that. And here you are, fresh again."

"What last time?"

"Master Kumnax," a mechanical voice interrupted.

He stood, looking down at her. "We glovers always have big mouths. They don't like us knowing, but once we know, what can they do about it?"

"You are in violation," the voice said. "Please report to S."

"But now, if you last, you'll know more than the tellman tells."

"I don't understand," Prufrax said slowly, precisely, looking him straight in the eye.

"I've paid my debt," Kumnax said. "We glovers stick. Now I'm going to go get my punishment." He left the cubicle. Prufrax didn't see him again before her first application.

The seedship buried itself in a heating protostar, raising shields against the infalling ice and stone. The nebula had congealed out of a particularly rich cluster of exploded fourth- and fifth-generation stars, thick with planets, the detritus of which now fell on Aryz's ship like hail.

Aryz had never been so isolated. No other branch ind addressed him; he never even saw them now. He made his reports to the brood mind, but even there the reception was warmer and warmer, until he could barely endure to communicate. Consequently—and he realized this was part of the plan—he came closer to his charges, the human shapes. He felt more sympathy for them. He discovered that even between human and Senexi there could be a bridge and need—the need to be useful.

The brood mind was interested in one question: how successfully could they be planted aboard a human ship? Would they be accepted until they could carry out their sabotage, or would they be detected? Already Senexi instructions were being coded into their teachings.

"I think they will be accepted in the confusion of an engagement," Aryz answered. He had long since guessed the general outlines of the brood mind's plans. Communication with the human shapes was for one purpose only: to use them as decoys, insurgents. They were weapons. Knowledge of human activity and behavior was not an end in itself; seeing what was happening to him, Aryz fully understood why the brood mind wanted such study to proceed no further.

He would lose them soon, he thought, and his work would be over. He would be much too human-tainted. He would end, and his replacement would start a new existence, very little different from Aryz—but, he reasoned, adjusted. The replacement would not have Aryz's peculiarity.

He approached his last meeting with the brood mind, preparing himself for his final work, for the ending. In the cold liquid-filled chamber, the great red-and-white sac waited, the center of his team, his existence. He adored it. There was no way he could criticize its action.

Yet—

"We are being sought," the brood mind radiated. "Are the shapes ready?"

"Yes," Aryz said. "The new teaching is firm. They believe they are fully human." And, except for the new teaching, they were. "They defy sometimes." He said nothing about the mutated shape. It would not be used. If they won this encounter, it would probably be placed with Aryz's body in a fusion torch for complete purging.

"Then prepare them," the brood mind said. "They will be delivered to the vector for positioning and transfer."

Darkness and waiting. Prufrax nested in her delivery tube like a freshly chambered round. Through her gloves she caught distant communications murmurs that resembled voices down hollow pipes. The *Mellangee* was coming to full readiness.

Huge as her ship was, Prufrax knew it would be dwarfed by the seedship. She could recall some hazy details about the seedship's structure, but most of that information was stored securely away from interference by her conscious mind. She wasn't even positive what the tactic would be. In the mocks, that at least had been clear. Now such information either had not been delivered or had waited in inaccessible memory, to be brought forward by the appropriate triggers.

More information would be fed to her just before

the launch, but she knew the general procedure. The
seedship was deep in a protostar, hiding behind the
distortion of geometry and the complete hash of
electromagnetic energy. The *Mellangee* would approach, collide if need be. Penetrate. Release. Find.
Zap. Her fingers ached. Sometime before the launch
she would also be fed her final moans—the tempers—
and she would be primed to leave elfstate. She would
be a mature glover. She would be a woman.

If she returned

will return

she could become part of the breed, her receptivity
would end in ecstasy rather than mild warmth, she
would contribute second state, naturally born glovers.
For a moment she was content with the thought. That
was a high honor.

Her fingers ached worse.

The tempers came, moans tiding in, then the battle
data. As it passed into her subconscious, she caught a
flash of—

Rocks and ice, a thick cloud of dust and gas
glowing red but seeming dark, no stars, no constellation guides this time. The beacon came on. That
would be her only way to orient once the gloves
stopped inertial and locked onto the target.

The seedship

was like

a shadow within a shadow

twenty-two kilometers across, yet

carrying

only six

teams

LAUNCH *She flies!*

Data: the *Mellangee* has buried herself in the seedship, ploughed deep into the interior like a carnivore's muzzle looking for vitals.

Instruction: a swarm of seeks is dashing through the seedship, looking for the brood minds, for the brood chambers, for branch inds. The glovers will follow.

Prufrax sees herself clearly now. She is the great avenging comet, bringer of omen and doom, like a knife moving through the glass and ice and thin, cold helium as if they weren't there, the chambered round fired and tearing at hundreds of kilometers an hour through the Senexi vessel, following the seeks.

The seedship cannot withdraw into higher geometries now. It is pinned by the *Mellangee*. It is hers.

Information floods her, pleases her immensely. She swoops down orange-and-grey corridors, buffeting against the walls like a ricocheting bullet. Almost immediately she comes across a branch ind, sliding through the ammonia film against the outrushing wind, trying to reach an armored cubicle. Her first Zap is too easy, not satisfying, nothing like what she thought. In her wake the branch ind becomes scattered globules of plasma. She plunges deeper.

Aryz delivers his human charges to the vectors that will launch them. They are equipped with simulations of the human weapons, their hands encased in the hideous grey gloves.

The seedship is in deadly peril; the battle has almost been lost at one stroke. The seedship cannot remain whole. It must self-destruct, taking the human ship with it, leaving only a fragment with as many teams as can escape.

The vectors launch the human shapes. Aryz tries to determine which part of the ship will be elected to survive; he must not be there. His job is over, and he must die.

The glovers fan out through the seedship's central hollow, demolishing the great cold drive engines, bypassing the shielded fusion flare and the reprocessing plant, destroying machinery built before their Earth was formed.

The special-projects sisters take the lead. Suddenly they are confused. They have found a brood mind, but it is not heavily protected. They surround it, prepare for the Zap—

It is sacrificing itself, drawing them in to an easy kill and away from another portion of the seedship. Power is concentrating elsewhere. Sensing that, they kill quickly and move on.

Aryz's brood mind prepares for escape. It begins to wrap itself in flux bind as it moves through the ship toward the frozen fragment. Already three of its five branch inds are dead; it can feel other brood minds dying. Aryz's bud replacement has been killed as well.

Following Aryz's training, the human shapes rush into corridors away from the main action. The special-projects sisters encounter the decoy male, allow it to fly with them . . . until it aims its weapons. One Zap almost takes out Trice. The others fire on the shape immediately. He goes to his death weeping, confused from the very moment of his launch.

The fragment in which the brood mind will take refuge encompasses the chamber where the humans had been nurtured, where the mandate is still stored. All the other brood minds are dead, Aryz realizes; the humans have swept down on them so quickly. What shall he do?

Somewhere, far off, he feels the distressed pulse of another branch ind dying. He probes the remains of the seedship. He is the last. He cannot dissipate now; he must ensure the brood mind's survival.

Prufrax, darting through the crumbling seedship, searching for more opportunities, comes across an injured glover. She calls for a mediseek and pushes on.

The brood mind settles into the fragment. Its support system is damaged; it is entering the time-isolated state, the flux bind, more rapidly than it should. The seals of foamed electric ice cannot quite close off the fragment before Ya, Trice, and Damu slip in. They frantically call for bind-cutters and preservers; they have instructions to capture the last brood mind, if possible.

But a trap falls upon Ya, and snarling fields tear her from her gloves. She is flung down a dark disintegrating shaft, red cracks opening all around as the seedship's integrity fails. She trails silver dust and freezes, hits a barricade, shatters.

The ice seals continue to close. Trice is caught between them and pushes out frantically, blundering into the region of the intensifying flux bind. Her gloves break into hard bits, and she is melded into an ice wall like an insect trapped on the surface of a winter lake.

Damu sees that the brood mind is entering the final

phase of flux bind. After that they will not be able to touch it. She begins a desperate Zap

and is too late.

Aryz directs the subsidiary energy of the flux against her. Her Zap deflects from the bind region, she is caught in an interference pattern and vibrates until her tiniest particles stop their knotted whirlpool spins and she simply becomes

space and searing light.

The brood mind, however, has been damaged. It is losing information from one portion of its anatomy. Desperate for storage, it looks for places to hold the information before the flux bind's last wave.

Aryz directs an interface onto the brood mind's surface. The silvery pools of time-binding flicker around them both. The brood mind's damaged sections transfer their data into the last available storage device—the human mandate.

Now it contains both human and Senexi information.

The silvery pools unite, and Aryz backs away. No longer can he sense the brood mind. It is out of reach but not yet safe. He must propel the fragment from the remains of the seedship. Then he must wrap the fragment in its own flux bind, cocoon it in physics to protect it from the last ravages of the humans.

Aryz carefully navigates his way through the few remaining corridors. The helium atmosphere has almost completely dissipated, even there. He strains to remember all the procedures. Soon the seedship will explode, destroying the human ship. By then they must be gone.

Angry red, Prufrax follows his barely sensed form, watching him behind barricades of ice, approaching the moment of a most satisfying Zap. She gives her gloves their way

and finds a shape behind her, wearing gloves that are not gloves, not like her own, but capable of grasping her in tensed fields, blocking the Zap, dragging them together. The fragment separates, heat pours in from the protostar cloud. They are swirled in their vortex of power, twin locked comets—one red, one sullen grey.

"Who are you?" Prufrax screams as they close in on each other in the fields. Their environments meld. They grapple. In the confusion, the darkening, they are drawn out of the cloud with the fragment, and she sees the other's face.

Her own.

The seedship self-destructs. The fragment is propelled from the protostar, above the plane of what will become planets in their orbits, away from the crippled and dying *Mellangee*.

Desperate, Prufrax uses all her strength to drill into the fragment. Helium blows past them, and bits of dead branch inds.

Aryz catches the pair immediately in the shapes chamber, rearranging the fragment's structure to enclose them with the mutant shape and mandate. For the moment he has time enough to concentrate on them. They are dangerous. They are almost equal to each other, but his shape is weakening faster than the true glover. They float, bouncing from wall to wall in the chamber, forcing the mutant to crawl into a corner and howl with fear.

There may be value in saving the one and capturing the other. Involved as they are, the two can be carefully dissected from their fields and induced into a crude kind of sleep before the glover has a chance to free her weapons. He can dispose of the gloves—fake and real—and hook them both to the Mam, reattach the mutant shape as well. Perhaps something can be learned from the failure of the experiment.

The dissection and capture occur faster than the planning. His movement slows under the spreading flux bind. His last action, after attaching the humans to the Mam, is to make sure the brood mind's flux bind is properly nested within that of the ship.

The fragment drops into simpler geometries.

It is as if they never existed.

The battle is over. There were no victors. Aryz became aware of the passage of time, shook away the sluggishness, and crawled through painfully dry corridors to set the environmental equipment going again. Throughout the fragment, machines struggled back to activity.

How many generations? The constellations were unrecognizable. He made star traces and found familiar spectra and types, but advanced in age. There had been a malfunction in the overall flux bind. He couldn't find the nebula where the battle had occurred. In its place were comfortably middle-aged stars surrounded by young planets.

Aryz came down from the makeshift observatory. He slid through the fragment, established the limits of his new home, and found the solid mirror surface of the brood mind's cocoon. It was still locked in flux bind, and he knew of no way to free it. In time the bind would probably wear off—but that might require life spans. The seedship was gone. They had lost the brood chamber, and with it the stock.

He was the last branch ind of his team. Not that it mattered now; there was nothing he could initiate without a brood mind. If the flux bind was permanent—as sometimes happened during malfunction—then he might as well be dead.

He closed his thought around him and was almost completely submerged when he sensed an alarm from the shapes chamber. The interface with the mandate had turned itself off; the new version of the Mam was malfunctioning. He tried to repair the equipment, but without the engineer's wall he was almost helpless. The best he could do was rig a temporary nutrition supply through the old human-form Mam. When he was done, he looked at the captive and the two shapes, then at the legless, armless Mam that served as their link to the interface and life itself.

She had spent her whole life in a room barely eight by ten meters, and not much taller than her own height. With her had been Grayd and the silent round creature whose name—if it had any—they had never learned. For a time there had been Mam, then another kind of Mam not nearly as satisfactory. She was hardly aware that her entire existence had been miserable, cramped, in one way or another incomplete.

Separated from them by a transparent partition, another round shape had periodically made itself known by voice or gesture.

Grayd had kept her sane. They had engaged in conspiracy. Removing themselves from the interface—what she called "eyes-shut"—they had held on to each other, tried to make sense out of what they knew instinctively, what was fed them through the interface, and what the being beyond the partition told them.

First they knew their names, and they knew that they were glovers. They knew that glovers were fighters. When Aryz passed instruction through the interface of how to fight, they had accepted it eagerly but uneasily. It didn't seem to jibe with instructions locked deep within their instincts.

Five years under such conditions had made her introspective. She expected nothing, sought little beyond experience in the eyes-shut. Eyes-open with Grayd seemed scarcely more than a dream. They usually managed to ignore the peculiar round creature in the chamber with them; it spent nearly all its time hooked to the mandate and the Mam.

Of one thing only was she completely sure. Her name was Prufrax. She said it in eyes-open and eyes-shut, her only certainty.

Not long before the battle, she had been in a condition resembling dreamless sleep, like a robot being given instructions. The part of Prufrax that had taken on personality during eyes-shut and eyes-open for five years had been superseded by the fight instructions Aryz had programmed. She had flown as glovers must fly (though the gloves didn't seem quite right). She had fought, grappling (she thought) with herself, but who could be certain of anything?

She had long since decided that reality was not to be sought too avidly. After the battle she fell back into the mandate—into eyes-shut—all too willingly.

And what matter? If eyes-open was even less comprehensible than eyes-shut, why did she have the nagging feeling eyes-open was so compelling, so necessary? She tried to forget.

But a change had come to eyes-shut, too. Before the battle, the information had been selected. Now she could wander through the mandate at will. She seemed to smell the new information, completely unfamiliar, like a whiff of ocean. She hardly knew where to begin. She stumbled across:

—that all vessels will carry one, no matter what their size or class, just as every individual carries the map of a species. The mandate shall contain all the information of our kind, including accurate and uncensored history, for if we have learned anything, it is that censored and untrue accounts distort the eyes of the leaders. Leaders must have access to the truth. It is their responsibility. Whatever is told those who work under the leaders, for whatever reasons, must not be believed by the leaders. Unders are told lies. Leaders must seek and be provided with accounts as accurate as possible, or we will be weakened and fall—

What wonderful dreams the *leaders* must have had. And they possessed some intrinsic gift called *truth*, through the use of the *mandate*. Prufrax could hardly believe that. As she made her tentative explorations through the new fields of eyes-shut, she began to link the word *mandate* with what she experienced. That was where she was.

And she alone. Once, she had explored with Grayd. Now there was no sign of Grayd.

She learned quickly. Soon she walked along a beach on Earth, then a beach on a world called Myriadne, and other beaches, fading in and out. By running through the entries rapidly, she came up with a blurred *eidos* and so learned what a beach was in the abstract. It was a boundary between one kind of eyes-shut and another, between water and land, neither of which had any corollary in eyes-open.

Some beaches had sand. Some had clouds—the *eidos* of clouds was quite attractive. And one—

had herself running scared, screaming.

She called out, but the figure vanished. Prufrax stood on a beach under a greenish-yellow star, on a world called Kyrene, feeling lonelier than ever.

She explored farther, hoping to find Grayd, if not the figure that looked like herself. Grayd wouldn't flee from her. Grayd would—

The round thing confronted her, its helpless limbs twitching. Now it was her turn to run, terrified. Never before had she met the round creature in eyes-shut. It was mobile; it had a purpose. Over land, clouds, trees, rocks, wind, air, equations, and an edge of physics she fled. The farther she went, the more distant from the round one with hands and small head, the less afraid she was.

She never found Grayd.

The memory of the battle was fresh and painful. She remembered the ache of her hands, clumsily removed from the gloves. Her environment had collapsed and been replaced by something indistinct. Prufrax had fallen into a deep slumber and had dreamed.

The dreams were totally unfamiliar to her. If there was a left-turning in her arc of sleep, she dreamed of philosophies and languages and other things she couldn't relate to. A right-turning led to histories and sciences so incomprehensible as to be nightmares.

It was a most unpleasant sleep, and she was not at all sorry to find she wasn't really asleep.

The crucial moment came when she discovered how to slow her turnings and the changes of dream subject. She entered a pleasant place of which she had no knowledge but which did not seem threatening. There was a vast expanse of water, but it didn't terrify her. She couldn't even identify it as water until she scooped up a handful. Beyond the water was a floor of shifting particles. Above both was an open expanse, not black but obviously space, drawing her eyes into intense pale blue-green. And there was that figure she had encountered in the seedship. Herself. The figure pursued. She fled.

Right over the boundary into Senexi information. She knew then that what she was seeing couldn't possibly come from within herself. She was receiving data from another source. Perhaps she had been taken captive. It was possible she was now being forcibly debriefed. The tellman had discussed such possibilities, but none of the glovers had been taught how to defend themselves in specific situations. Instead it had been stated—in terms that brooked no second thought—that self-destruction was the only answer. So she tried to kill herself.

She sat in the freezing cold of a red-and-white room, her feet meeting but not touching a fluid covering on the floor. The information didn't fit her senses—it seemed blurred, inappropriate. Unlike the other data, this didn't allow participation or motion. Everything was locked solid.

She couldn't find an effective means of killing herself. She resolved to close her eyes and simply will herself into dissolution. But closing her eyes only moved her into a deeper or shallower level of deception—other categories, subjects, visions. She couldn't sleep, wasn't tired, couldn't die.

Like a leaf on a stream, she drifted. Her thoughts untangled, and she imagined herself floating on the water called ocean. She kept her eyes open. It was quite by accident that she encountered:

Instruction. Welcome to the introductory use of the mandate. As a noncombat processor, your duties are to maintain the mandate, provide essential information for your overs, and, if necessary, protect or destroy the mandate. The mandate is your immediate over. If it requires maintenance, you will oblige. Once linked with the mandate, as you are now, you may explore any aspect of the information by requesting delivery. To request delivery, indicate the core of your subject—

Prufrax! she shouted silently. What is Prufrax?

A voice with different tone immediately took over.

Ah, now that's quite a story. I was her biographer, the organizer of her life tapes (ref. GEORGE MACKNAX), and knew her well in the last years of her life. She was born in the Ferment 26468. Here are

selected life tapes. Choose emphasis. Analyses follow.

—Hey! Who are you? There's someone here with me. . . .

—Shh! Listen. Look at her. Who is she?

They looked, listened to the information.

—Why, she's *me* . . . sort of.

—She's *us*.

She stood two and a half meters tall. Her hair was black and thick, though cut short; her limbs well-muscled though drawn out by the training and hormonal treatments. She was seventeen years old, one of the few birds born in the solar system, and for the time being she had a chip on her shoulder. Everywhere she went, the birds asked about her mother, Jayax. "You better than her?"

Of course not! Who could be? But she was good; the instructors said so. She was just about through training, and whether she graduated to hawk or remained bird she would do her job well. Asking Prufrax about her mother was likely to make her set her mouth tight and glare.

On Mercior, the Grounds took up four thousand hectares and had its own port. The Grounds was divided into Land, Space, and Thought, and training in each area was mandatory for fledges, those birds embarking on hawk training. Prufrax was fledge three. She had passed Land—though she loathed downbound fighting—and was two years into Space. The tough part, everyone said, was not passing Space, but lasting through four years of Thought after the action in nearorbit and planetary.

Prufrax was not the introspective type. She could be studious when it suited her. She was a quick study at weapon maths, physics came easy when it had a direct application, but theory of service and polinstruc—which she had sampled only in prebird courses—bored her.

Since she had been a little girl, no more than five——Five! Five what?

and had seen her mother's ships and fightsuits and fibs, she had known she would never be happy until she had ventured far out and put a seedship in her sights, had convinced a Senexi of the overness of end—

—The Zap! She's talking the Zap!

—What's that?

—You're me, you should know.

—I'm not you, we're not her.

The Zap, said the mandate, and the data shifted.

"Tomorrow you receive your first implants. These will allow you to coordinate with the zero-angle phase engines and find your targets much more rapidly than you ever could with simple biologic. The implants, of course, will be delivered through your noses—minor irritation and sinus trouble, no more—into your limbic system. Later in your training, hookups and digital adapts will be installed as well. Are there any questions?"

"Yes, sir." Prufrax stood at the top of the spherical classroom, causing the hawk instructor to swivel his platform. "I'm having problems with the zero-angle phase maths. Reduction of the momenta of the real."

Other fledge threes piped up that they, too, had had trouble with those maths. The hawk instructor sighed. "We don't want to install cheaters in all of you. It's bad enough needing implants to supplement biologic. Individual learning is much more desirable. Do you request cheaters?" That was a challenge. They all responded negatively, but Prufrax had a secret smile. She knew the subject. She just took delight in having the maths explained again. She could reinforce an already thorough understanding. Others not so well versed would benefit. She wasn't wasting time. She was in the pleasure of her weapon—the weapon she would be using against the Senexi.

"Zero-angle phase is the temporary reduction of the momenta of the real." Equations and plexes appeared before each student as the instructor went on. "Nested unreals can conflict if a barrier is placed between the participator princip and the assumption of the real. The effectiveness of the participator can be determined by a convenience model we call the angle of phase. Zero-angle phase is achieved by an opaque probability field according to modified Fourier of the separation of real waves. This can also be caused by the reflection of the beam—an effective counter to zero-angle phase, since the beam is always compoundable and the compound is always time-reversed. Here are the true gedanks—"

—Zero-angle phase. She's learning the Zap.

—She hates them a lot, doesn't she?

—The Senexi? They're Senexi.

—I think . . . eyes-open is the world of the Senexi What does that mean?

—That we're prisoners. You were caught before me.

—Oh.

The news came as she was in recovery from the implant. Seedships had violated human space again, dropping cuckoos on thirty-five worlds. The worlds had been young colonies, and the cuckoos had wiped out all life, then tried to reseed with Senexi forms. The overs had reacted by sterilizing the planet's surfaces. No victory, loss to both sides. It was as if the Senexi were so malevolent they didn't care about success, only about destruction.

She hated them. She could imagine nothing worse.

Prufrax was twenty-three. In a year she would be qualified to hawk on a cruiser/raider. She would demonstrate her hatred.

Aryz felt himself slipping into endthought, the mind set that always preceded a branch ind's self-destruction. What was there for him to do? The fragment had survived, but at what cost, to what purpose? Nothing had been accomplished. The nebula had been lost, or he supposed it had. He would likely never know the actual outcome.

He felt a vague irritation at the lack of a spectrum of responses. Without a purpose, a branch ind was nothing more than excess plasm.

He looked in on the captive and the shapes, all hooked to the mandate, and wondered what he would do with them. How would humans react to the situation he was in? More vigorously, probably. They would fight on. They always had. Even without leaders, with no discernible purpose, even in defeat. What gave them such stamina? Were they superior, more deserving? If they were better, then was it right for the Senexi to oppose their triumph?

Aryz drew himself tall and rigid with confusion. He had studied them too long. They had truly infected him. But here at least was a hint of purpose. A question needed to be answered.

He made preparations. There were signs the brood mind's flux bind was not permanent, was in fact unwinding quite rapidly. When it emerged, Aryz would present it with a judgment, an answer.

He realized, none too clearly, that by Senexi standards he was now a raving lunatic.

He would hook himself into the mandate, improve the somewhat isolating interface he had used previously to search for selected answers. He, the captive, and the shapes would be immersed in human history together. They would be like young suckling on a Population I mother-animal—just the opposite of the Senexi process, where young fed nourishment and information into the brood mind.

The mandate would nourish, or poison. Or both.

—Did she love?

—What—you mean, did she receive?

—No, did she—we—I—give?

—I don't know what you mean.

—I wonder if *she* would know what I mean. . . .

Love, said the mandate, and the data proceeded.

Prufrax was twenty-nine. She had been assigned to a cruiser in a new program where superior but untested fighters were put into thick action with no preliminary. The program was designed to see how well the Grounds prepared fighters; some thought it foolhardy, but Prufrax found it perfectly satisfactory.

The cruiser was a million-ton raider, with a hawk contingent of fifty-three and eighty regular crew. She would be in a second-wave attack, following the initial hardfought.

She was scared. That was good; fright improved basic biologic, if properly managed. The cruiser would make a raid into Senexi space and retaliate for past cuckoo-seeding programs. They would come up against thornships and seedships, likely.

The fighting was going to be fierce.

The raider made its final denial of the overness of the real and pip-squeezed into an arduous, nasty sponge space. It drew itself together again and emerged far above the galactic plane.

Prufrax sat in the hawks wardroom and looked at the simulated rotating snowball of stars. Red-coded numerals flashed along the borders of known Senexi territory, signifying old stars, dark hulks of stars, the whole ghostly home region where they had first come to power when the terrestrial sun had been a mist-wrapped youngster. A green arrow showed the position of the raider.

She drank sponge-space supplements with the others but felt isolated because of her firstness, her fear. Everyone seemed so calm. Most were fours or fives—on their fourth or fifth battle call. There were ten ones and an upper scatter of experienced hawks with nine to twenty-five battles behind them. There were no thirties. Thirties were rare in combat; the few that survived so many engagements were plucked off active and retired to PR service under the polinstructors. They often ended up in fibs, acting poorly, looking unhappy.

Still, when she had been more naive, Prufrax's heroes had been a man-and-woman thirty team she had watched in fib after fib—Kumnax and Arol. They had been better actors than most.

Day in, day out, they drilled in their fightsuits. While the crew bustled, hawks were put through implant learning, what slang was already calling the Know, as opposed to the Tell, of classroom teaching. Getting background, just enough to tickle her curiosity, not enough to stimulate morbid interest.

—There it is again. Feel?

—I know it. Yes. The round one, part of eyes-open . . .

—Senexi?

—No, brother without name.

—Your . . . brother?

—No . . . I don't know.

—Can it hurt us?

—It never has. It's trying to talk to us.

—*Leave us alone!*

—It's going.

Still, there were items of information she had never received before, items privileged only to the fighters, to assist them in their work. Older hawks talked about the past, when data had been freely available. Stories circulated in the wardroom about the Senexi, and she managed to piece together something of their origins and growth.

Senexi worlds, according to a twenty, had originally
been large, cold masses of gas circling bright young
suns nearly metal-free. Their gas-giant planets had
orbited the suns at hundreds of millions of kilometers
and had been dusted by the shrouds of neighboring
dead stars; the essential elements carbon, nitrogen,
silicon, and fluorine had gathered in sufficient quan-
tities on some of the planets to allow Population II
biology.

In cold ammonia seas, lipids had combined in
complex chains. A primal kind of life had arisen and
flourished. Across millions of years, early Senexi
forms had evolved. Compared with evolution on
Earth, the process at first had moved quite rapidly.
The mechanisms of procreation and evolution had
been complex in action, simple in chemistry.

There had been no competition between life forms
of different genetic bases. On Earth, much time had
been spent selecting between the plethora of possible
ways to pass on genetic knowledge.

And among the early Senexi, outside of predation
there had been no death. Death had come about much
later, self-imposed for social reasons. Huge colonies
of protoplasmic individuals had gradually resolved
into the team-forms now familiar.

Soon information was transferred through the bud-
ding of branch inds; cultures quickly developed to
protect the integrity of larvae, to allow them to
regroup and form a new brood mind. Technologies
had been limited to the rare heavy materials available,
but the Senexi had expanded for a time with very little
technology. They were well adapted to their environ-

ment, with few predators and no need to hunt,
absorbing stray nutrients from the atmosphere and
from layers of liquid ammonia. With perceptions
attuned to the radio and microwave frequencies, they
had before long turned groups of branch inds into
radio telescope chains, piercing the heavy atmosphere
and probing the universe in great detail, especially the
very active center of the young galaxy. Huge jets of
matter, streaming from other galaxies and emitting
high-energy radiation, had provided laboratories for
their vicarious observations. Physics was a primitive
science to them.

Since little or no knowledge was lost in breeding
cycles, cultural growth was rapid at times; since the
dead weight of knowledge was often heavy, cultural
growth often slowed to a crawl.

Using water, as a building material, developing
techniques that humans still understood imperfectly,
they prepared for travel away from their birthworlds.

Prufrax wondered, as she listened to the older
hawks, how humans had come to know all this. Had
Senexi been captured and questioned? Was it all
theory? Did anyone really know—anyone she could
ask?

—She's weak.

—Why weak?

—Some knowledge is best for glovers to ignore.
Some questions are best left to the supreme overs.

—Have you thought that in here, you can answer
her questions, our questions?

—No. No. Learn about me—us—first.

In the hour before engagement, Prufrax tried to find

a place alone. On the raider this wasn't difficult. The ship's size was overwhelming for the number of hawks and crew aboard. There were many areas where she could put on an environs and walk or drift in silence, surrounded by the dark shapes of equipment wrapped in plexerv. There was so much about ship operations she didn't understand, hadn't been taught. Why carry so much excess equipment, weapons—far more than they'd need even for replacements? She could think of possibilities—superiors on Mercior wanting their cruisers to have flexible mission capabilities, for one—but her ignorance troubled her less than *why* she was ignorant. Why was it necessary to keep fighters in the dark on so many subjects?

She pulled herself through the cold G-less tunnels, feeling slightly awked by the loneness, the quiet. One tunnel angled outboard, toward the hull of the cruiser. She hesitated, peering into its length with her environs beacon, when a beep warned her she was near another crew member. She was startled to think someone else might be as curious as she. The other hawks and crew, for the most part, had long outgrown their need to wander and regarded it as birdish. Prufrax was used to being different—she had always perceived herself, with some pride, as a bit of a freak. She scooted expertly up the tunnel, spreading her arms and tucking her legs as she would in a fightsuit.

The tunnel was filled with a faint milky green mist, absorbing her environs beam. It couldn't be much more than a couple of hundred meters long, however, and it was quite straight. The signal beeped louder.

Ahead she could make out a dismantled weapons

blister. That explained the fog: a plexerv aerosol diffused in the low pressure. Sitting in the blister was a man, his environs glowing a pale violet. He had deopaqued a section of the blister and was staring out at the stars. He swiveled as she approached and looked her over dispassionately. He seemed to be a hawk—he had fightform, tall, thin with brown hair above hull-white skin, large eyes with pupils so dark she might have been looking through his head into space beyond.

"Under," she said as their environs met and merged.

"Over. What are you doing here?"

"I was about to ask you the same."

"You should be getting ready for the fight," he admonished.

"I am. I need to be alone for a while."

"Yes." He turned back to the stars. "I used to do that, too."

"You don't fight now?"

He shook his head. "Retired. I'm a researcher."

She tried not to look impressed. Crossing rates was almost impossible. A bitalent was unusual in the service.

"What kind of research?" she asked.

"I'm here to correlate enemy finds."

"Won't find much of anything, after we're done with the zero phase."

It would have been polite for him to say, "Power to that," or offer some other encouragement. He said nothing.

"Why would you want to research them?"

"To fight an enemy properly, you have to know what they are. Ignorance is defeat."

"You research tactics?"

"Not exactly."

"What, then?"

"You'll be in a tough hardfought this wake. Make you a proposition. You fight well, observe, come to me and tell me what you see. Then I'll answer your questions."

"Brief you before my immediate overs?"

"I have the authority," he said. No one had ever lied to her; she didn't even suspect he would. "You're eager?"

"Very."

"You'll be doing what?"

"Engaging Senexi fighters, then hunting down branch inds and brood minds."

"How many fighters going in?"

"Twelve."

"Big target, eh?"

She nodded.

"While you're there, ask yourself—what are they fighting for? Understand?"

"I—"

"Ask, what are they fighting for. Just that. Then come back to me."

"What's your name?"

"Not important," he said. "Now go."

She returned to the prep center as the sponge-space warning tones began. Overhawks went among the fighters in the lineup, checking gear and giveaway body points for mental orientation. Prufrax submitted to the molded sensor mask being slipped over her face. "Ready!" the overhawk said. "Hardfought!" He clapped her on the shoulder. "Good luck."

"Thank you, sir." She bent down and slid into her fightsuit. Along the launch line, eleven other hawks did the same. The overs and other crew left the chamber, and twelve red beams delineated the launch tube. The fightsuits automatically lifted and aligned on their individual beams. Fields swirled around them like silvery tissue in moving water, then settled and hardened into cold scintillating walls, pulsing as the launch energy built up.

The tactic came to her. The ship's sensors became part of her information net. She saw the Senexi thornship—twelve kilometers in diameter, cuckoos lacing its outer hull like maggots on red fruit, snakes waiting to take them on.

She was terrified and exultant, so worked up that her body temperature was climbing. The fightsuit adjusted her balance.

At the count of ten and nine, she switched from biologic to cyber. The implant—after absorbing much of her thought processes for weeks—became Prufrax.

For a time there seemed to be two of her. Biologic continued, and in that region she could even relax a bit, as if watching a fib.

With almost dreamlike slowness, in the electronic time of cyber, her fightsuit followed the beam. She saw the stars and oriented herself to the cruiser's beacon, using both for reference, plunging in the sword-flower formation to assault the thornship. The cuckoos retreated in the vast red hull like worms withdrawing into an apple. Then hundreds of tiny black pinpoints appeared in the closest quadrant to the sword flower.

Snakes shot out, each piloted by a Senexi branch
ind. "Hardfought!" she told herself in biologic before
that portion gave over completely to cyber.

Why were we flung out of dark
through ice and fire, a shower
of sparks? a puzzle;
Perhaps to build hell.

We strike here, there;
Set brief glows, fall through
and cross round again.

By our dimming, we see what
Beatitude we have.

In the circle, kindling
together, we form an
exhausted Empyrean.
We feel the rush of
igniting winds but still
grow dull and wan.

New rage flames, new light,
dropping like sun through muddy
ice and night and fall
Close, spinning blue and bright.
In time they, too,
Tire. Redden.
We join, compare pasts
cool in huddled paths,
turn grey.

And again.
We are a companion flow
of ash, in the slurry,
out and down.
We sleep.

Rivers form above and below.
Above, iron snakes twist,
clang and slice, chime,
helium eyes watching, seeing
Snowflake hawks,
signaling adamant muscles and
energy teeth. What hunger
compels our venom spit?

It flies, strikes the crystal
flight, making mist grey-green
with ammonia rain.

Sleeping, we glide,
and to each side
unseen shores wait
with the moans of an
unseen tide.

—She wrote that. We. One of her—our—poems.
—Poem?
—A kind of fib, I think.
—I don't see what it says.
—Sure you do! She's talking hardfought.
—The Zap? Is that all?
—No, I don't think so.

—Do you understand it?

—Not all . . .

She lay back in the bunk, legs crossed, eyes closed, feeling the receding dominance of the implant—the overness of cyber—and the almost pleasant ache in her back. She had survived her first. The thornship had retired, severely damaged, its surface seared and scored so heavily it would never release cuckoos again.

It would become a hulk, a decoy. Out of action. *Satisfaction/out of action/Satisfaction* . . .

Still, with eight of the twelve fighters lost, she didn't quite feel the exuberance of the rhyme. The snakes had fought very well. Bravely, she might say. They lured, sacrificed, cooperated, demonstrating teamwork as fine as that in her own group. Strategy was what made the cruiser's raid successful. A superior approach, an excellent tactic. And perhaps even surprise, though the final analysis hadn't been posted yet.

Without those advantages, they might have all died.

She opened her eyes and stared at the pattern of blinking lights in the ceiling panel, lights with their secret codes that repeated every second, so that whenever she looked at them, the implant deep inside was debriefed, reinstructed. Only when she fought would she know what she was now seeing.

She returned to the tunnel as quickly as she was able. She floated up toward the blister and found him there, surrounded by packs of information from the last hardfought. She waited until he turned his attention to her.

"Well?" he said.

"I asked myself what they are fighting for. And I'm very angry."

"Why?"

"Because I don't know. I *can't* know. They're Senexi."

"Did they fight well?"

"We lost eight. Eight." She cleared her throat.

"Did they fight well?" he repeated, an edge in his voice.

"Better than I was ever told they could."

"Did they die?"

"Enough of them."

"How many did you kill?"

"I don't know." But she did. Eight.

"You killed eight," he said, pointing to the packs. "I'm analyzing the battle now."

"You're behind what we read, what gets posted?" she asked.

"Partly," he said. "You're a good hawk."

"I knew I would be," she said, her tone quiet, simple.

"Since they fought bravely—"

"How can Senexi be brave?" she asked sharply.

"Since," he repeated, "they fought bravely, why?"

"They want to live, to do their . . . work. Just like me."

"No," he said. She was confused, moving between extremes in her mind, first resisting, then giving in too much. "They're Senexi. They're not like us."

"What's your name?" she asked, dodging the issue.

"Clevo."

Her glory hadn't even begun yet, and already she was well into her fall.

Aryz made his connection and felt the brood mind's emergency cache of knowledge in the mandate grow up around him like ice crystals on glass. He stood in a static scene. The transition from living memory to human machine memory had resulted in either a coding of data or a reduction of detail; either way, the memory was cold, not dynamic. It would have to be compared, recorrelated, if that would ever be possible.

How much human data had had to be dumped to make space for this?

He cautiously advanced into the human memory, calling up topics almost at random. In the short time he had been away, so much of what he had learned seemed to have faded or become scrambled. Branch inds were supposed to have permanent memory; human data, for one reason or another, didn't take. It required so much effort just to begin to understand the different modes of thought.

He backed away from sociological data, trying to remain within physics and mathematics. There he could make conversions to fit his understanding without too much strain.

Then something unexpected happened. He felt the brush of another mind, a gentle inquiry from a source made even stranger by the hint of familiarity. It made what passed for a Senexi greeting, but not in the proper form, using what one branch ind of a team would radiate to a fellow; a gross breach, since it was obviously not from his team or even from his family.

Aryz tried to withdraw. How was it possible for minds to meet in the mandate? As he retreated, he pushed into a broad region of incomprehensible data. It had none of the characteristics of the other human regions he had examined.

—This is for machines, the other said. —Not all cultural data is limited to biologic. You are in the area where programs and cyber designs are stored. They are really accessible only to a machine hooked into the mandate.

—What is your family? Aryz asked, the first step-question in the sequence Senexi used for urgent identity requests.

—I have no family. I am not a branch ind. No access to active brood minds. I have learned from the mandate.

—Then what are you?

—I don't know, exactly. Not unlike you.

Aryz understood what he was dealing with. It was the mind of the mutated shape, the one that had remained in the chamber, beseeching when he approached the transparent barrier.

—I must go now, the shape said. Aryz was alone again in the incomprehensible jumble. He moved slowly, carefully, into the Senexi sector, calling up subjects familiar to him. If he could encounter one shape, doubtless he could encounter the others—perhaps even the captive.

The idea was dreadful—and fascinating. So far as he knew, such intimacy between Senexi and human had never happened before. Yet there was something very Senexi-like in the method, as if branch inds attached to the brood mind were to brush mentalities while searching in the ageless memories.

The dread subsided. There was little worse that could happen to him, with his fellows dead, his brood mind in flux bind, his purpose uncertain.

What Aryz was feeling, for the first time, was a small measure of *freedom*.

The story of the original Prufrax continued.

In the early stages she visited Clevo with a barely concealed anger. His method was aggravating, his goals never precisely spelled out. What did he want with her, if anything?

And she with him? Their meetings were clandestine, though not precisely forbidden. She was a hawk one now with considerable personal liberty between exercises and engagements. There were no monitors in the closed-off reaches of the cruiser, and they could do whatever they wished. The two met in areas close to the ship's hull, usually in weapons blisters that could be opened to reveal the stars; there they talked.

Prufrax was not accustomed to prolonged conversation. Hawks were not raised to be voluble, nor were they selected for their curiosity. Yet the exhawk Clevo talked a great deal and was the most curious person she had met, herself included, and she regarded herself as uncharacteristically curious.

Often he was infuriating, especially when he played the "leading game," as she called it. Leading her from one question to the next like an instructor, but without the trappings of any clarity of purpose. "What do you think of your mother?"

"Does that matter?"

"Not to me."

"Then why ask?"

"Because you matter."

Prufrax shrugged. "She was a fine mother. She bore me with a well-chosen heritage. She raised me as a hawk candidate. She told me her stories."

"Any hawk I know would envy you for listening at Jay-ax's knee."

"I was hardly at her knee."

"A speech tactic."

"Yes, well, she was important to me."

"She was a preferred single?"

"Yes."

"So you have no father."

"She selected without reference to individuals."

"Then you are really not that much different from a Senexi."

She bristled and started to push away. "There! You insult me again."

"Not at all. I've been asking one question all this time, and you haven't even heard. How well do you know the enemy?"

"Well enough to destroy them." She couldn't believe that was the only question he'd been asking. His speech tactics were very odd.

"Yes, to win battles, perhaps. But who will win the war?"

"It'll be a long war," she said softly, floating a few meters from him. He rotated in the blister, blocking out a blurred string of stars. The cruiser was preparing to shift out of status geometry again. "They fight well."

"They fight with conviction. Do you believe them to be evil?"

"They destroy us."

"We destroy them."

"So the question," she said, smiling at her cleverness, "is who began to destroy?"

"Not at all," Clevo said. "I suspect there's no longer a clear answer to that. Our leaders have obviously decided the question isn't important. No. We are the new, they are the old. The old must be superseded. It's a conflict born in the essential difference between Senexi and humans."

"That's the only way we're different? They're old, we're not so old? I don't understand."

"Nor do I, entirely."

"Well, finally!"

"The Senexi," Clevo continued, unperturbed, "long ago needed only gas-giant planets like their homeworlds. They lived in peace for billions of years before our world was formed. But as they moved from star to star, they learned uses for other types of worlds. We were most interested in rocky Earth-like planets. Gradually, we found uses for gas giants, too. By the time we met, both of us encroached on the other's territory. Their technology is so improbable, so unlike ours, that when we first encountered them, we thought they must come from another geometry."

"Where did you learn all this?" Prufrax squinted at him suspiciously.

"I'm no longer a hawk," he said, "but I was too valuable just to discard. My experience was too broad, my abilities too useful. So I was placed in research. It seems a safe place for me. Little contact with my comrades." He looked directly at her. "We must try to know our enemy, at least a little."

"That's dangerous," Prufrax said, almost instinctively.

"Yes, it is. What you know, you cannot hate."

"We must hate," she said. "It makes us strong. Senexi hate."

"They might," he said. "But, sometime, wouldn't you like to . . . sit down and talk with one, after a battle Talk with a fighter? Learn its tactic, how it bested you in one move, compare—"

"No!" Prufrax shoved off rapidly down the tube. "We're shifting now. We have to get ready."

—She's smart. She's leaving him. He's crazy.

—Why do you think that?

—He would stop the fight, end the Zap.

—But he was a hawk.

—And hawks became glovers, I guess. But glovers go wrong, too. Like you.

—?

—Did you know they used you? How you were used?

—That's all blurred now.

—She's doomed if she stays around him. Who's that?

—Someone is listening with us.

—Recognize?

—No, gone now.

The next battle was bad enough to fall into the hellfought. Prufrax was in her fightsuit, legs drawn up as if about to kick off. The cruiser exited sponge space

and plunged into combat before sponge-space supplements could reach full effectiveness. She was dizzy,
disoriented. The overhawks could only hope that a
switch from biologic to cyber would cure the problem.

She didn't know what they were attacking. Tactic
was flooding the implant, but she was only receiving
the wash of that; she hadn't merged yet. She sensed
that things were confused. That bothered her. Overs
did not feel confusion.

The cruiser was taking damage. She could sense at
least that, and she wanted to scream in frustration.
Then she was ordered to merge with the implant.
Biologic became cyber. She was in the Know.

The cruiser had reintegrated above a gas-giant
planet. They were seventy-nine thousand kilometers
from the upper atmosphere. The damage had come
from ice mines—chunks of Senexi-treated water ice,
altered to stay in sponge space until a human vessel
integrated nearby. Then they emerged, packed with
momentum and all the residual instability of an
unsuccessful exit into status geometry. Unsuccessful
for a ship, that is—very successful for a weapon.

The ice mines had given up the overness of the real
within range of the cruiser and had blasted out whole
sections of the hull. The launch lanes had not been
damaged. The fighters lined up on their beams and
were peppered out into space, spreading in the classic
sword flower.

The planet was a cold nest. Over didn't know what
the atmosphere contained, but Senexi activity had
been high in the star system, concentrating on this
world. Over had decided to take a chance. Fighters

headed for the atmosphere. The cruiser began planting singularity eggs. The eggs went ahead of the fighters, great black grainy ovoids that seemed to leave a trail of shadow—the wake of a birthing disruption in status geometry that could turn a gas giant into a short-lived sun.

Their time was limited. The fighters would group on entry sleds and descend to the liquid water regions where Senexi commonly kept their upwelling power plants. The fighters would first destroy any plants, loop into the liquid ammonia regions to search for hidden cuckoos, then see what was so important about the world.

She and five other fighters mounted the sled. Growing closer, the hazy clear regions of the atmosphere sparkled with Senexi sensors. Spiderweb beams shot from the six sleds to down the sensors. Buffet began. Scream, heat, then a second flower from the sled at a depth of two hundred kilometers. The sled slowed and held station. It would be their only way back. The fightsuits couldn't pull out of such a large gravity well.

She descended deeper. The pale, bloated beacon of the red star was dropping below the second cloudtops, limning the strata in orange and purple. At the liquid ammonia level she was instructed to key in permanent memory of all she was seeing. She wasn't "seeing" much, but other sensors were recording a great deal, all of it duly processed in her implant. "There's life here," she told herself. Indigenous life. Just another example of Senexi disregard for basic decency: they were interfering with a world developing its own complex biology.

The temperature rose to ammonia vapor levels, then to liquid water. The pressure on the fightsuit was enormous, and she was draining her stores much more rapidly than expected. At this level the atmosphere was particularly thick with organics.

Senexi snakes rose from below, passed them in altitude, then doubled back to engage. Prufrax was designated the deep diver; the others from her sled would stay at this level in her defense. As she fell, another sled group moved in behind her to double the cover.

She searched for the characteristic radiation curve of an upwelling plant. At the lower boundary of the liquid water level, below which her suit could not safely descend, she found it.

The Senexi were tapping the gas giant's convection from greater depths than usual. Above the plant, almost indetectable, was another object with an uncharacteristic curve. They were separated by ten kilometers. The power plant was feeding its higher companion with tight energy beams.

She slowed. Two other fighters, disengaged from the brief skirmish above, took positions as backups a few dozen kilometers higher than she. Her implant searched for an appropriate tactic. She would avoid the zero-angle phase for the moment, go in for reconnaissance. She could feel sound pouring from the plant and its companion—rhythmic, not waste noise, but deliberate. And homing in on that sound were waves of large vermiform organisms, like chains of gas-filled sausage. They were dozens of meters long, two meters at their greatest thickness, shaped vaguely like the Senexi snake fighters. The vermiforms were native, and they were being lured into the uppermost floating structure. None were emerging. Her backups spread apart, descending, and drew up along her flanks.

She made her decision almost immediately. She could see a pattern in the approach of the natives. If she fell into the pattern, she might be able to enter the structure unnoticed.

—It's a grinder. She doesn't recognize it.

—What's a grinder?

—She should make the Zap! It's an ugly thing; Senexi use them all the time. Net a planet with grinders, like a cuckoo, but for larger operations.

The creatures were being passed through separator fields. Their organics fell from the bottom of the construct, raw material for new growth—Senexi growth. Their heavier elements were stored for later harvest.

With Prufrax in their midst, the vermiforms flew into the separator. The interior was hundreds of meters wide, lead-white walls with flat grey machinery floating in a dust haze, full of hollow noise, the distant bleats of vermiforms being slaughtered. Prufrax tried to retreat, but she was caught in a selector field. Her suit bucked and she was whirled violently, then thrown into a repository for examination. She had been screened from the separator; her plan to record, then destroy, the structure had been foiled by an automatic filter.

"Information sufficient." Command logic programmed into the implant before launch was now taking over. "Zero-angle phase both plant and adjunct." She was drifting in the repository, still slightly stunned. Something was fading. Cyber was hissing in and out; the over logic-commands were being scrambled. Her implant was malfunctioning and was returning control to biologic. The selector fields had played havoc with all cyber functions, down to the processors in her weapons.

Cautiously she examined the down systems one by one, determining what she could and could not do. This took as much as thirty seconds—an astronomical time on the implant's scale.

She still could use the phase weapon. If she was judicious and didn't waste her power, she could cut her way out of the repository, maneuver and work with her escorts to destroy both the plant and the separator. By the time they returned to the sleds, her implant might have rerouted itself and made sufficient repairs to handle defense. She had no way of knowing what was waiting for her if—when—she escaped, but that was the least of her concerns for the moment.

She tightened the setting of the phase beam and swung her fightsuit around, knocking a cluster of junk ice and silty phosphorescent dust. She activated the beam. When she had a hole large enough to pass through, she edged the suit forward, beamed through more walls and obstacles, and kicked herself out of the repository into free fall. She swiveled and laid down a pattern of wide-angle beams, at the same time relaying a message on her situation to the escorts.

The escorts were not in sight. The separator was beginning to break up, spraying debris through the almost-opaque atmosphere. The rhythmic sound ceased and the crowds of vermiforms began to disperse.

She stopped her fall and thrust herself several kilometers higher—directly into a formation of Senexi snakes. She had barely enough power to reach the sled, much less fight and turn her beams on the upwelling plant.

Her cyber was still down.

The sled signal was weak. She had no time to calculate its direction from the inertial guidance cyber. Besides, all cyber was unreliable after passing through the separator.

Why do they fight so well? Clevo's question clogged her thoughts. Cursing, she tried to blank and keep all her faculties available for running the fightsuit. *When evenly matched, you cannot win against your enemy unless you understand them. And if you truly understand, why are you fighting and not talking?* Clevo had never told her that— not in so many words. But it was part of a string of logic all her own.

Be more than an automaton with a narrow range of choices. Never underestimate the enemy. Those were old Grounds dicta, not entirely lost in the new training, but only emphasized by Clevo.

If they fight as well as you, perhaps in some ways they fight-think like you do. Use that.

Isolated, with her power draining rapidly, she had no choice. They might disregard her if she posed no danger. She cut her thrust and went into a diving spin. Clearly she was on her way to a high-pressure grave. They would sense her power levels, perhaps even pick up the lack of field activity if she let her shields drop.

She dropped the shields. If they let her fall and didn't try to complete the kill—if they concentrated on active fighters above—she had enough power to drop into the water vapor regions, far below the plant, and silently ride a thermal into range. With luck, she could get close enough to lay a web of zero-angle phase and take out the plant.

She had minutes in which to agonize over her plan. Falling, buffeted by winds that could knock her kilometers out of range, she spun like a vagrant flake of snow.

She couldn't even expend the energy to learn if they were scanning her, checking out her potential.

Perhaps she underestimated them. Perhaps they would be that much more thorough and take her out just to be sure. Perhaps they had unwritten rules of conduct like the ones she was using, taking hunches into account. Hunches were discouraged in Grounds training—much less reliable than cyber.

She fell. Temperature increased. Pressure on her suit began to constrict her air supply. She used fighter trancing to cut back on her breathing.

Fell.

And broke the trance. Pushed through the dense smoke of exhaustion. Planned the beam web. Counted her reserves. Nudged into an updraft beneath the plant. The thermal carried her, a silent piece of paper in a storm, drifting back and forth beneath the objective. The huge field intakes pulsed above, lightning outlining their invisible extension. She held back on the beam.

Nearly faded out. Her suit interior was almost unbearably hot.

She was only vaguely aware of laying down the pattern. The beams vanished in the murk. The thermal pushed her through a layer of haze, and she saw the plant, riding high above clear-atmosphere turbulence. The zero-angle phase had pushed through the field intakes, into their source nodes and the plant body, surrounding it with bright blue Tcherenkov. First the surface began to break up, then the middle layers, and finally key supports. Chunks vibrated away with the internal fury of their molecular, then atomic, then particle disruption. Paraphrasing Grounds description of beam action, the plant became less and less convinced of its reality. "Matter dreams," an instructor had said a decade before. "Dreams it is real, maintains the dream by shifting rules with constant results. Disturb the dreams, the shifting of the rules results in inconstant results. Things cannot hold."

She slid away from the updraft, found another, wondered idly how far she would be lifted. Curiosity at the last. Let's just see, she told herself; a final experiment.

Now she was cold. The implant was flickering, showing signs of reorganization. She didn't use it. No sense expanding the amount of time until death. No sense—

at all.

The sled, maneuvered by one remaining fighter, glided up beneath her almost unnoticed.

Aryz waited in the stillness of a Senexi memory, his thinking temporarily reduced to a faint susurrus. What he waited for was not clear.

—Come.

The form of address was wrong, but he recognized the voice. His thoughts stirred, and he followed the nebulous presence out of Senexi territory.

—Know your enemy.

Prufrax . . . the name of one of the human shapes sent out against their own kind. He could sense her presence in the mandate, locked into a memory store. He touched on the store and caught the essentials—the grinder, the updraft plant, the fight from Prufrax's viewpoint.

—Know how your enemy knows you.

He sensed a second presence, similar to that of Prufrax. It took him some time to realize that the human captive was another form of the shape, a reproduction of the . . .

Both were reproductions of the female whose image was in the memory store. Aryz was not impressed by threes—Senexi mysticism, what had ever existed of it, had been preoccupied with fives and sixes—but the coincidence was striking.

—Know how your enemy *sees* you.

He saw the grinder processing organics—the vermiform natives—in preparation for a widespread seeding of deuterium gatherers. The operation had evidently been conducted for some time; the vermiform populations were greatly reduced from their usual numbers. Vermiforms were a common type-species on gas giants of the sort depicted. The mutated shape nudged him into a particular channel of the memory, that which carried the original Prufrax's emotions. She had reacted with *disgust* to the Senexi procedure. It was a reaction not unlike what Aryz might feel when coming across something forbidden in Senexi behavior. Yet eradication was perfectly natural, analogous to the human cleansing of *food* before *eating*.

—It's in the memory. The vermiforms are intelligent. They have their own kind of civilization. Human action on this world prevented their complete extinction by the Senexi.

—So what matter they were *intelligent?* Aryz responded. They did not behave or think like Senexi, or like any species Senexi find compatible. They were therefore not desirable. Like humans.

—You would make humans extinct?

—We would protect ourselves from them.

—Who damages whom most?

Aryz didn't respond. The line of questioning was incomprehensible. Instead he flowed into the memory of Prufrax, propelled by another aspect of complete freedom, confusion.

The implant was replaced. Prufrax's damaged limbs and skin were repaired or regenerated quickly, and within four wakes, under intense treatment usually reserved only for overs, she regained all her reflexes and speed. She requested liberty of the cruiser while it returned for repairs. Her request was granted.

She first sought Clevo in the designated research area. He wasn't there, but a message was, passed on to her by a smiling young crew member. She read it quickly:

"You're free and out of action. Study for a while,

then come find me. The old place hasn't been damaged. It's less private, but still good. Study! I've marked highlights."

She frowned at the message, then handed it to the crew member, who duly erased it and returned to his duties. She wanted to talk with Clevo, not study.

But she followed his instructions. She searched out highlighted entries in the ship's memory store. It was not nearly as dull as she had expected. In fact, by following the highlights, she felt she was learning more about Clevo and about the questions he asked.

Old literature was not nearly as graphic as fibs, but it was different enough to involve her for a time. She tried to create imitations of what she read, but erased them. Nonfib stories were harder than she suspected. She read about punishment, duty; she read about places called heaven and hell, from a writer who had died tens of thousands of years before. With ed supplement guidance, she was able to comprehend most of what she read. Plugging the store into her implant, she was able to absorb hundreds of volumes in an hour.

Some of the stores were losing definition. They hadn't been used in decades, perhaps centuries.

Halfway through, she grew impatient. She left the research area. Operating on another hunch, she didn't go to the blister as directed, but straight to memory central, two decks inboard the research area. She saw Clevo there, plugged into a data pillar, deep in some aspect of ship history. He noticed her approach, unplugged, and swiveled on his chair. "Congratulations," he said, smiling at her.

"Hardfought," she acknowledged, smiling.

"Better than that, perhaps," he said.

She looked at him quizzically. "What do you mean, better?"

"I've been doing some illicit tapping on over channels."

"So?"

—He *is dangerous!*

"You've been recommended."

"For what?"

"Not for hero status, not yet. You'll have a good many more fights before that. And you probably won't enjoy it when you get there. You won't be a fighter then."

Prufrax stood silently before him.

"You may have a valuable genetic assortment. Overs think you behaved remarkably well under impossible conditions."

"Did I?"

He nodded. "Your type may be preserved."

"Which means?"

"There's a program being planned. They want to take the best fighters and reproduce them—clone them—to make uniform topgrade squadrons. It was rumored in my time—you haven't heard?"

She shook her head.

"It's not new. It's been done, off and one, for tens of thousands of years. This time they believe they can make it work."

"You were a fighter, once," she said. "Did they preserve your type?"

Clevo nodded. "I had something that interested them, but not, I think, as a fighter."

Prufrax looked down at her stubby-fingered hands. "It was grim," she said. "You know what we found?"

"An extermination plant."

"You want me to understand them better. Well, I can't. I refuse. How could they do such things?" She looked disgusted and answered her own question. "Because they're Senexi."

"Humans," Clevo said, "have done much the same, sometimes worse."

"No!"

—No!

"Yes," he said firmly. He sighed. "We've wiped Senexi worlds, and we've even wiped worlds with intelligent species like our own. Nobody is innocent. Not in this universe."

"We were never taught that."

"It wouldn't have made you a better hawk. But it might make a better human of you, to know. Greater depth of character. Do you want to be more aware?"

"You mean, study more?"

He nodded.

"What makes you think *you* can teach me?"

"Because you thought about what I asked you. About how Senexi thought. And you survived where some other hawk might not have. The overs think it's in your genes. It might be. But it's also in your head.

"Why not tell the overs?"

"I have," he said. He shrugged. "I'm too valuable to them, otherwise, I'd have been busted again, a long time ago."

"They wouldn't want me to learn from you?"

"I don't know," Clevo said. "I suppose they're

aware you're talking to me. They could stop it if they wanted. They may be smarter than I give them credit for." He shrugged again. "Of course they're smart. We just disagree at times."

"And if I learn from you?"

"Not from me, actually. From the past. From history, what other people have thought. I'm really not any more capable than you . . . but I know history, small portions of it. I won't teach you so much, as guide."

"I did use your questions," Prufrax said. "But will I ever need to use them—think that way—again?"

Clevo nodded. "Of course."

—You're quiet.

—She's giving in to him.

—She gave in a long time ago.

—She should be afraid.

—Were you—we—ever really afraid of a challenge?

—No.

—Not Senexi, not forbidden knowledge.

—Someone listens with us. Feel—

Clevo first led her through the history of past wars, judging that that was appropriate considering her occupation. She was attentive enough, though her mind wandered; sometimes he was didactic, but she found that didn't bother her much. At no time did his attitude change as they pushed through the tangle of the past. Rather her perception of his attitude changed. Her perception of herself changed.

She saw that in all wars, the first stage was to dehumanize the enemy, reduce the enemy to a lower level so that he might be killed without compunction. When the enemy was not human to begin with, the task was easier. As wars progressed, this tactic frequently led to an underestimation of the enemy, with disastrous consequences. "We aren't exactly underestimating the Senexi," Clevo said. "The overs are too smart for that. But we refuse to understand them, and that could make the war last indefinitely."

"Then why don't the overs see that?"

"Because we're being locked into a pattern. We've been fighting for so long, we've begun to lose ourselves. And it's getting worse." He assumed his didactic tone, and she knew he was reciting something he'd formulated years before and repeated to himself a thousand times. "There is no war so important that to win it, we must destroy our minds."

She didn't agree with that; losing the war with the Senexi would mean extinction, as she understood things.

Most often they met in the single unused weapons blister that had not been damaged. They met when the ship was basking in the real between sponge-space jaunts. He brought memory stores with him in portable modules, and they read, listened, experienced together. She never placed a great deal of importance in the things she learned; her interest was focused on Clevo. Still, she learned.

The rest of her time she spent training. She was aware of a growing isolation from the hawks, which she attributed to her uncertain rank status. Was her genotype going to be preserved or not? The decision hadn't been made. The more she learned, the less she wanted to be singled out for honor. Attracting that sort of attention might be dangerous, she thought. Dangerous to whom, or what, she could not say.

Clevo showed her how hero images had been used to indoctrinate birds and hawks in a standard of behavior that was ideal, not realistic. The results were not always good; some tragic blunders had been made by fighters trying to be more than anyone possibly could or refusing to be flexible.

The war was certainly not a fib. Yet more and more the overs seemed to be treating it as one. Unable to bring about strategic victories against the Senexi, the overs had settled in for a long war of attrition and were apparently bent on adapting all human societies to the effort.

"There are overs we never hear of, who make decisions that shape our entire lives. Soon they'll determine whether or not we're even born, if they don't already."

"That sounds paranoid," she said, trying out a new word and concept she had only recently learned.

"Maybe so."

"Besides, it's been like that for ages—not knowing all our overs."

"But it's getting worse," Clevo said. He showed her the projections he had made. In time, if trends continued unchanged, fighters and all other combatants would be treated more and more mechanically, until they became the machines the overs wished them to be.

—No.

—Quiet. How does he feel toward her?

It was inevitable that as she learned under his tutelage, he began to feel responsible for her changes. She was an excellent fighter. He could never be sure that what he was doing might reduce her effectiveness. And yet he had fought well—despite similar changes—until his billet switch. It had been the overs who had decided he would be more effective, less disruptive, elsewhere.

Bitterness over that decision was part of his motive. The overs had done a foolish thing, putting a fighter into research. Fighters were tenacious. If the truth was to be hidden, then fighters were the ones likely to ferret it out. And pass it on. There was a code among fighters, seldom revealed to their immediate overs, much less to the supreme overs parsecs distant in their strategospheres. What one fighter learned that could be of help to another had to be passed on, even under penalty. Clevo was simply following that unwritten rule.

Passing on the fact that, at one time, things had been different. That war changed people, governments, societies, and that societies could effect an enormous change on their constituents, especially now—change in their lives, their thinking. Things could become even more structured. Freedom of fight was a drug, an illusion—

—No!

used to perpetuate a state of hatred.

"Then why do they keep all the data in stores?" she asked. "I mean, you study the data, everything becomes obvious."

"There are still important people who think we may

want to find our way back someday. They're afraid we'll lose our roots, but—"

His face suddenly became peaceful. She reached out to touch him, and he jerked slightly, turning toward her in the blister. "What is it?" she asked.

"It's not organized. We're going to lose the information. Ship overs are going to restrict access more and more. Eventually it'll decay, like some already has in these stores. I've been planning for some time to put it all in a single unit—"

—He built the mandate!

"and have the overs place one on every ship, with researchers to tend it. Formalize the loose scheme still in effect, but dying. Right now I'm working on the fringes. At least I'm allowed to work. But soon I'll have enough evidence that they won't be able to argue. Evidence of what happens to societies that try to obscure their histories. They go quite mad. The overs are still rational enough to listen; maybe I'll push it through." He looked out the transparent blister. The stars were smudging to one side as the cruiser began probing for entrances to sponge space. "We'd better get back."

"Where are you going to be when we return? We'll all be transferred."

"That's some time removed. Why do you want to know?"

"I'd like to learn more."

He smiled. "That's not your only reason."

"I don't need someone to tell me what my reasons are," she said testily.

"We're so reluctant," he said. She looked at him

sharply, irritated and puzzled. "I mean," he continued, "we're hawks. Comrades. Hawks couple like
that." He snapped his fingers. "But you and I sneak
around it all the time."

Prufrax kept her face blank.

"Aren't you receptive toward me?" he asked, his
tone almost teasing.

"You're so damned superior. Stuffy," she snapped.

"Aren't you?"

"It's just that's not all," she said, her tone soften-
ing.

"Indeed," he said in a barely audible whisper.

In the distance they heard the alarms.

—It was never any different.

—What?

—Things were never any different before me.

—Don't be silly. It's all here.

—If Clevo made the mandate, then he put it here. It
isn't true.

—Why are you upset?

—I don't like hearing that everything I believe is
a . . . fib.

—I've never known the difference, I suppose.
Eyes-open was never all that real to me. This isn't
real, you aren't . . . this is eyes-shut. So why be
upset? You and I . . . we aren't even whole people.
I feel you. You wish the Zap, you fight, not much
else. I'm just a shadow, even compared to you. But
she is whole. She loves him. She's less a victim than
either of us. So something has to have changed.

—You're saying things have gotten worse.

—If the mandate is a lie, that's all I am. You refuse

to accept. I *have* to accept, or I'm even less than a shadow.

—I don't refuse to accept. It's just hard.

—You started it. You thought about love.

—You did!

—Do you know what love is?

—Reception.

They first made love in the weapons blister. It came as no surprise; if anything, they approached it so cautiously they were clumsy. She had become more and more receptive, and he had dropped his guard. It had been quick, almost frantic, far from the orchestrated and drawn-out ballet the hawks prided themselves for. There was no pretense. No need to play the roles of artists interacting. They were depending on each other. The pleasure they exchanged was nothing compared to the emotions involved.

"We're not very good with each other," Prufrax said.

Clevo shrugged. "That's because we're shy."

"Shy?"

He explained. In the past—at various times in the past, because such differences had come and gone many times—making love had been more than a physical exchange or even an expression of comradeship. It had been the acknowledgment of a bond between people.

She listened, half-believing. Like everything else she had heard, that kind of love seemed strange, distasteful. What if one hawk was lost, and the other continued to love? It interfered with the hardfought, certainly. But she was also fascinated. Shyness—the fear of one's presentation to another. The hesitation to present truth, or the inward confusion of truth at the awareness that another might be important, more important than one thought possible. That such emotions might have existed at one time, and seem so alien now, only emphasized the distance of the past, as Clevo had tried to tell her. And that she felt those emotions only confirmed she was not as far from that past as, for dignity's sake, she might have wished.

Complex emotion was not encouraged either at the Grounds or among hawks on station. Complex emotion degraded complex performance. The simple and direct was desirable.

"But all we seem to do is talk—until now," Prufrax said, holding his hand and examining his fingers one by one. They were very little different from her own, though extended a bit from hawk fingers to give greater versatility with key instruction.

"Talking is the most human thing we can do."

She laughed. "I know what you are," she said, moving up until her eyes were even with his chest. "You're stuffy. You aren't the party type."

"Where'd you learn about parties?"

"You gave me literature to read, I read it. You're an instructor at heart. You make love by telling." She felt peculiar, almost afraid, and looked up at his face. "Not that I don't enjoy your lovemaking, like this. Physical."

"You receive well," he said. "Both ways."

"What we're saying," she whispered, "is not truth-speaking. It's amenity." She turned into the stroke of his hand through her hair. "Amenity is supposed to be decadent. That fellow who wrote about heaven and hell. He would call it a sin."

"Amenity is the recognition that somebody may see or feel differently than you do. It's the recognition of individuals. You and I, we're part of the end of all that."

"Even if you convince the overs?"

He nodded. "They want to repeat success without risk. New individuals are risky, so they duplicate past success. There will be more and more people, fewer individuals. More of you and me, less of others. The fewer individuals, the fewer stories to tell. The less history. We're part of the death of history."

She floated next to him, trying to blank her mind as she had before, to drive out the nagging awareness that he was right. She thought she understood the social structure around her. Things seemed new. She said as much.

"It's a path we're taking," Clevo said. "Not a place we're at."

—It's a place *we're* at. How different are *we*?

—But there's so much history in here. How can it be over for us?

—I've been thinking. Do we know the last event recorded in the mandate?

—Don't, we're drifting from Prufrax now. . . .

Aryz felt himself drifting with them. They swept over countless millennia, then swept back the other way. And it became evident that as much change had been wrapped in one year of the distant past as in a thousand years of the closing entries in the mandate. Clevo's voice seemed to follow them, though they were far from his period, far from Prufrax's record.

"Tyranny is the death of history. We fought the

Senexi until we became like them. No change, youth
at an end, old age coming upon us. There is no
important change, merely elaborations in the pattern."

—How many times have we been here, then? How
many times have we died?

Aryz wasn't sure, now. *Was* this the first time
humans had been captured? Had he been told everything by the brood mind? Did the Senexi have no
history, whatever that was—

**The accumulated lives of living, thinking beings.
Their actions, thoughts, passions, hopes.**

The mandate answered even his confused, nonhu-
man requests. He could understand action, thought,
but not passion or hope. Perhaps without those there
was no *history*.

—You have no history, the mutated shape told him.
There have been millions like you, even millions like
the brood mind. What is the last event recorded in the
brood mind that is not duplicated a thousand times
over, so close they can be melded together for convenience?

—You understand that? Aryz asked the shape.

—Yes.

—How do you understand—because we made you
between human and Senexi?

—Not only that.

The requests of the twins, captive and shape, were
moving them back once more into the past, through
the dim grey millennia of repeating ages. History
began to manifest again, differences in the record.

On the way back to Mercior, four skirmishes were
fought. Prufrax did well in each. She carried some-

thing special with her, a thought she didn't even tell Clevo, and she carried the same thought with her through their last days at the Grounds.

Taking advantage of hawk liberty, she opted a posthardfought residence just outside the Grounds, in the relatively uncrowded Daughter of Cities zone. She wouldn't be returned to fight until several issues had been decided—her status most important among them.

Clevo began making his appeal to the middle overs. He was given Grounds duty to finish his proposals. They could stay together for the time being.

The residence was sixteen square meters in area, not elegant—*natural*, as rentOpts described it. Clevo called it a "garret," inaccurately as she discovered when she looked it up in his memory blocs, but perhaps he was describing the tone.

On the last day she lay in the crook of Clevo's arm. They had done a few hours of nature sleep. He hadn't come out yet, and she looked up at his face, reached up with a hand to feel his arm.

It was different from the arms of others she had been receptive toward. It was unique. The thought amused her. There had never been a reception like theirs. This was the beginning. And if both were to be duplicated, this love, this reception, would be repeated an infinite number of times. Clevo meeting Prufrax, teaching her, opening her eyes.

Somehow, even though repetition contributed to the death of history, she was pleased. This was the secret thought she carried into fight. Each time she would survive, wherever she was, however many duplications down the line. She would receive Clevo, and he would teach her. If not now—if one or the other died—then in the future. The death of history might be a good thing. Love could go on forever.

She had lost even a rudimentary apprehension of death, even with present pleasure to live for. Her functions had sharpened. She would please him by doing all the things he could not. And if he was to enter that state she frequently found him in, that state of introspection, of reliving his own battles and envying her activity, then that wasn't bad. All they did to each other was good.

—*Was* good

—*Was*

She slipped from his arm and left the narrow sleeping quarter, pushing through the smoke-colored air curtain to the lounge. Two hawks and an over she had never seen before were sitting there. They looked up at her.

"Under," Prufrax said.

"Over," the woman returned. She was dressed in tan and green. Grounds colors, not ship.

"May I assist?"

"Yes."

"My duty, then?"

The over beckoned her closer. "You have been receiving a researcher."

"Yes," Prufrax said. The meetings could not have been a secret on the ship, and certainly not their quartering near the Grounds. "Has that been against duty?"

"No." The over eyed Prufrax sharply, observing her perfected fightform, the easy grace with which she stood, naked, in the middle of the small compartment. "But a decision has been reached. Your status is decided now."

She felt a shiver.

"Prufrax," said the elder hawk. She recognized him from fibs, and his companion: Kumnax and Arol. Once her heroes. "You have been accorded an honor, just as your partner has. You have a valuable genetic assortment—"

She barely heard the rest. They told her she would return to fight, until they deemed she had had enough experience and background to be brought into the polinstruc division. Then her fighting would be over. She would serve better as an example, a hero.

Clevo emerged from the air curtain. "Duty," the over said. "The residence is disbanded. Both of you will have separate quarters, separate duties."

They left. Prufrax held out her hand, but Clevo didn't take it. "No use," he said.

Suddenly she was filled with anger. "You'll give it up? Did I expect too much? *How strongly?*"

"Perhaps even more strongly than you," he said. "I knew the order was coming down. And still I didn't leave. That may hurt my chances with the supreme overs."

"Then at least I'm worth more than your breeding history?"

"Now you are history. History the way they make it."

"I feel like I'm dying," she said, amazement in her voice. "What is that, Clevo? What did you do to me?"

"I'm in pain, too," he said.

"You're hurt?"

"I'm confused."

"I don't believe that," she said, her anger rising again. "You knew, and you didn't do anything?"

"That would have been counter to duty. We'll be worse off if we fight it."

"So what good is your great, exalted history?"

"History is what you have," Clevo said. "I only record."

—Why did they separate them?

—I don't know. You didn't like him, anyway.

—Yes, but now . . .

—See? You're her. We're her. But shadows. She was whole.

—I don't understand.

—We don't. Look what happens to her. They took what was best out of her. Prufrax

went into battle eighteen more times before dying as heroes often do, dying in the midst of what she did best. The question of what made her better before the separation—for she definitely was not as fine a fighter after—has not been settled. Answers fall into an extinct classification of knowledge, and there are few left to interpret, none accessible to this device.

—So she went out and fought and died. They never even made fibs about her. This killed her?

—I don't think so. She fought well enough. She died like other hawks died.

—And she might have lived otherwise.

—How can I know that, any more than you?

—They—we—met again, you know. I met a Clevo

once, on my ship. They didn't let me stay with him
long.

—How did you react to him?

—There was so little time, I don't know.

—Let's ask. . . .

**In thousands of duty stations, it was inevitable
that some of Prufrax's visions would come true,
that they should meet now and then. Clevos were
numerous, as were Prufraxes. Every ship carried
complements of several of each. Though Prufrax
was never quite as successful as the original, she
was a fine type. She—**

—She was never quite as successful. They took
away her edge. They didn't even know it!

—They must have known.

—Then they didn't want to win!

—We don't know that. Maybe there were more
important considerations.

—Yes, like killing history.

Aryz shuddered in his warming body, dizzy as if
about to bud, then regained control. He had been
pulled from the mandate, called to his own duty.

He examined the shapes and the human captive.
There was something different about them. How long
had they been immersed in the mandate? He checked
quickly, frantically, before answering the call. The
reconstructed Mam had malfunctioned. None of them
had been nourished. They were thin, pale, cooling.

Even the bloated mutant shape was dying; lost, like
the others, in the mandate.

He turned his attention away. Everything was confusion. Was he human or Senexi now? Had he fallen

so low as to understand them? He went to the origin of the call, the ruins of the temporary brood chamber. The corridors were caked with ammonia ice, burning his pod as he slipped over them. The brood mind had come out of flux bind. The emergency support systems hadn't worked well; the brood mind was damaged.

"Where have you been?" it asked.

"I assumed I would not be needed until your return from the flux bind."

"You have not been watching!"

"Was there any need? We are so advanced in time, all our actions are obsolete. The nebula is collapsed, the issue is decided."

"We do not know that. We are being pursued."

Aryz turned to the sensor wall—what was left of it—and saw that they were, indeed, being pursued. He had been lax.

"It is not your fault," the brood mind said. "You have been set a task that tainted you and ruined your function. You will dissipate."

Aryz hesitated. He had become so different, so tainted, that he actually *hesitated* at a direct command from the brood mind. But it was damaged. Without him, without what he had learned, what could it do? It wasn't reasoning correctly.

"There are facts you must know, important facts— "

Aryz felt a wave of revulsion, uncomprehending fear, and something not unlike human anger radiate from the brood mind. Whatever he had learned and however he had changed, he could not withstand that wave.

Willingly, and yet against his will—it didn't matter—he felt himself liquefying. His pod slumped beneath him, and he fell over, landing on a pool of frozen ammonia. It burned, but he did not attempt to lift himself. Before he ended, he saw with surprising clarity what it was to be a branch ind, or a brood mind, or a human. Such a valuable insight, and it leaked out of her permea and froze on the ammonia.

The brood mind regained what control it could of the fragment. But there were no defenses worthy of the name. Calm, preparing for its own dissipation, it waited for the pursuit to conclude.

The Mam set off an alarm. The interface with the mandate was severed. Weak, barely able to crawl, the humans looked at each other in horror and slid to opposite corners of the chamber.

They were confused: which of them was the captive, which the decoy shape? It didn't seem important. They were both bone-thin, filthy with their own excrement. They turned with one motion to stare at the bloated mutant. It sat in its corner, tiny head incongruous on the huge thorax, tiny arms and legs barely functional even when healthy. It smiled wanly at them.

"We felt you," one of the Prufraxes said. "You were with us in there." Her voice was a soft croak.

"That was my place," it replied. "My own place."

"What function, what name?"

"I'm . . . I know that. I'm a researcher. In there. I knew myself in there."

They squinted at the shape. The head. Something familiar, even now. "You're a Clevo . . ."

There was noise all around them, cutting off the shape's weak words. As they watched, their chamber was sectioned like an orange, and the wedges peeled open. The illumination ceased. Cold enveloped them.

A naked human female, surrounded by tiny versions of herself, like an angel circled by fairy kin, floated into the chamber. She was thin as a snake. She wore nothing but silver rings on her wrists and a narrow torque around her waist. She glowed blue-green in the dark.

The two Prufraxes moved their lips weakly but made no sound in the near vacuum. *Who are you?*

She surveyed them without expression, then held out her arms as if to fly. She wore no gloves, but she was of their type.

As she had done countless times before on finding such Senexi experiments—though this seemed older than most—she lifted one arm higher. The blue-green intensified, spread in waves to the mangled walls, surrounded the freezing, dying shapes. Perfect, angelic, she left the debris behind to cast its fitful glow and fade.

They had destroyed every portion of the fragment but one. They left it behind unharmed.

Then they continued, millions of them thick like mist, working the spaces between the stars, their only master the overness of the real.

They needed no other masters. They would never malfunction.

The mandate drifted in the dark and cold, its memory going on, but its only life the rapidly fading tracks where minds had once passed through it. The trails writhed briefly, almost as if alive, but only following the quantum rules of diminishing energy states. Finally, a small memory was illuminated.

Prufrax's last poem, explained the mandate reflexively.

> How the fires grow! Peace passes
> All memory lost.
> Somehow we always miss that single door
> Dooming ourselves to circle.
>
> Ashes to stars, lies to souls,
> Let's spin round the sinks and holes.
>
> Kill the good, eat the young.
> Forever and more
> You and I are never done.

The track faded into nothing. Around the mandate, the universe grew old very quickly.

I WILL NEVER UNDERSTAND

how the first person to test the drive made it past this point. The images silently surrounding me a bare arm's length away were lifesize, lifelike, and as solid as the panels and chairs they seemed to have displaced.

ALL OF THEM WERE ME.

Five seconds later the second set of images appeared, perfectly aligned with the first. After that they came more and more quickly. I watched—forced myself to watch— knew I *had* to watch—as the lines continued to lengthen.

I TOOK A LONG, SHUDDERING BREATH.

You don't have to look, I told myself, eyes rigidly fixed on the back of the image in front of me. *You've seen it all before*. But I'd fought this fight before and knew I would lose. Bracing myself, I turned my head and gazed down the line of images strung out to my left. Somehow, this space links us into alternate realities, universes that might have been if things had gone differently . . . I was seeing images of what I would be doing in each of those universes.

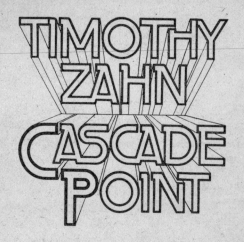

TIMOTHY ZAHN
CASCADE POINT

A TOM DOHERTY ASSOCIATES BOOK
NEW YORK

Reprinted by permission of the author and his agent, Scott Meredith
Literary Agency.

CASCADE POINT

A TOR Book
Published by Tom Doherty Associates, Inc.
49 West 24 Street
New York, NY 10010

Cover art by Tim White

ISBN: 0-812-55971-1   Can. ISBN: 0-812-55951-7

First edition: November 1988

Printed in the United States of America

0 9 8 7 6 5 4 3 2 1

In retrospect, I suppose I should have realized my number had come up on the universe's list right from the very start, right from the moment it became clear that I was going to be stuck with the job of welcoming the *Aura Dancer's* latest batch of passengers aboard. Still, I suppose it's just as well it was me and not Tobbar who let Rik Bradley and his psychiatrist onto my ship. There are some things that a captain should have no one to blame for but himself, and this was definitely in that category.

Right away I suppose that generates a lot of false impressions. A star liner captain, resplendent in white and gold, smiling toothily at elegantly dressed men and women as the ramp carries them through the polished entry portal—forget all of that. A tramp starmer isn't polished anywhere it doesn't absolutely have to be, the captain is lucky if he's got a clean jumpsuit—let alone some pseudomilitary Christmas tree frippery—and the passengers we get are the steerage of the star-traveling community. And look it.

Don't get me wrong; I have nothing against passengers aboard my ship. As a matter of fact, putting extra cabins in the *Dancer* had been my idea to start with, and they'd all too often made the difference between profit and loss in our always marginal business. But one of the reasons I had gone into space in the first place was to avoid having to make small talk with

strangers, and I would rather solo through four cascade points in a row than spend those agonizing minutes at the entry portal. In this case, though, I had no choice. Tobbar, our master of drivel—and thus the man unofficially in charge of civilian small talk—was up to his elbows in grease and balky hydraulics; and my second choice, Alana Keal, had finally gotten through to an equally balky tower controller who wanted to bump us ten ships back in the lift pattern. Which left exactly one person—me—because there was no one else *I'd* trust with giving a good first impression of my ship to paying customers. And so I was the one standing on the ramp when Bradley and his eleven fellow passengers hoved into sight.

They ranged from semiscruffy to respectable-but-not-rich—about par for the *Dancer*—but even in such a diverse group Bradley stood out like a red light on the status board. He was reasonably good-looking, reasonably average in height and build; but there was something in the way he walked that immediately caught my attention. Sort of a cross between nervous fear and something I couldn't help but identify as swagger. The mix was so good that it was several seconds before it occurred to me how mutually contradictory the two impressions were, and the realization left me feeling more uncomfortable than I already did.

Bradley was eighth in line, with the result that my first seven greetings were carried out without a lot of attention from my conscious mind—which I'm sure only helped. Even standing still, I quickly discovered, Bradley's strangeness made itself apparent, both in his

posture and also in his face and eyes. Especially his eyes.

Finally it was his turn at the head of the line. "Good morning, sir," I said, shaking his hand. "I'm Captain Pall Durriken. Welcome aboard."

"Thank you." His voice was bravely uncertain, the sort my mother used to describe as mousy. His eyes flicked the length of the *Dancer*, darted once into the portal, and returned to my face. "How often do ships like this crash?" he asked.

I hadn't expected any questions quite so blunt, but the fact that it was outside the realm of small talk made it easy to handle. "Hardly ever," I told him. "The last published figures showed a death rate of less than one per million passengers. You're more likely to be hit by a chunk of roof tile off the tower over there."

He actually cringed, turning halfway around to look at the tower. I hadn't dreamed he would take my comment so seriously, but before I could get my mouth working the man behind Bradley clapped a reassuring hand on his shoulder. "It's all right, Rik—nothing's going to hurt you. Really. This is a good ship, and we're going to be perfectly safe aboard her."

Bradley slowly straightened, and the other man shifted his attention to me. "I'm Dr. Hammerfeld Lanton, Captain," he said, extending his hand. "This is Rik Bradley. We're traveling in adjoining cabins."

"Of course," I said, nodding as if I'd already known that. In reality I hadn't had time to check out the passenger lists and assignments, but I could trust Leeds to have set things up properly. "Are you a doctor of medicine, sir?"

"In a way," Lanton said. "I'm a psychiatrist."

"Ah," I said, and managed two or three equally brilliant conversational gems before the two of them moved on. The last three passengers I dispatched with similar polish, and when everyone was inside I sealed the portal and headed for the bridge.

Alana had finished dickering with the tower and was running the prelift computer check when I arrived. "What's the verdict?" I asked as I slid into my chair and keyed for helm check.

"We've still got our lift slot," she said. "That's conditional on Matope getting the elevon system working within the next half hour, of course."

"Idiots," I muttered. The elevons wouldn't be needed until we arrived at Taimyr some six weeks from now, and Matope could practically rebuild them from scratch in that amount of time. To insist they be in prime condition before we could lift was unreasonable even for bureaucrats.

"Oh, there's no problem—Tobbar reported they were closing things up a few minutes ago. They'll put it through its paces, it'll work perfectly, they'll transmit the readout, and that'll be that." She cleared her throat. "Incidentally . . . are you aware we've got a skull-diver and his patient aboard?"

"Yes; I met—*patient*?" I interrupted myself as the last part of her sentence registered. "Who?"

"Name's Bradley," she said. "No further data on him, but apparently he and this Lanton character had a fair amount of electronic and medical stuff delivered to their cabins."

A small shiver ran up my back as I remembered

Bradley's face. No wonder he'd struck me as strange. "No mention at all of what's wrong—of why Bradley needs a psychiatrist?"

"Nothing. But it can't be anything serious." The test board bleeped, and Alana paused to peer at the results. Apparently satisfied, she keyed in the next test on the check list. "The Swedish Psychiatric Institute seems to be funding the trip, and they presumably know the regulations about notifying us of potential health risks."

"Um." On the other hand, a small voice whispered in my ear, if there was some problem with Bradley that made him marginal for space certification, they were more likely to get away with slipping him aboard a tramp than on a liner. "Maybe I should give them a call, anyway. Unless you'd like to?"

I glanced over in time to see her face go stony. "No, thank you," she said firmly.

"Right." I felt ashamed of the comment, not really having meant it the way it had come out. All of us had our own reasons for being where we were; Alana's was an overdose of third-degree emotional burns. She was the type who'd seemingly been born to nurse broken wings and bruised souls, the type who by necessity kept her own heart full view of both friends and passersby. Eventually, I gathered, one too many of her mended souls had torn out the emotional IVs she'd set up and flown off without so much as a backward glance, and she had renounced the whole business and run off to space. Ice to Europa, I'd thought once; there were enough broken wings out here for a whole shipload of Florence Nightingales.

But what I'd expected to be a short vacation for her had become four years' worth of armor plate over her emotions, until I wasn't sure she even knew anymore how to care for people. The last thing in the universe she would be interested in doing would be getting involved in any way with Bradley's problems. "Is all the cargo aboard now?" I asked, to change the subject.

"Yes, and Wilkinson certifies it's properly stowed."

"Good." I got to my feet. "I guess I'll make a quick spot survey of the ship, if you can handle things here."

"Go ahead," she said, not bothering to look up. Nodding anyway, I left.

I stopped first at the service shafts where Matope and Tobbar were just starting their elevon tests, staying long enough to satisfy myself the resulting data were adequate to please even the tower's bit-pickers. Then it was to each of the cargo holds to double-check Wilkinson's stowing arrangement, to the passenger area to make sure all their luggage had been properly brought on board, to the computer room to look into a reported malfunction—a false alarm, fortunately—and finally back to the bridge for the lift itself. Somehow, in all the running around, I never got around to calling Sweden. Not, as I found out later, that it would have done me any good.

We lifted right on schedule, shifting from the launch field's grav booster to ramjet at ten kilometers and kicking in the fusion drive as soon as it was legal to do so. Six hours later we were past Luna's orbit and ready for the first cascade maneuver.

Leeds checked in first, reporting officially that the

proper number of dosages had been drawn from the sleeper cabinet and were being distributed to the passengers. Pascal gave the okay from the computer room, Matope from the engine room, and Sarojis from the small chamber housing the field generator itself. I had just pulled a hard copy of the computer's course instructions when Leeds called back. "Captain, I'm in Dr. Lanton's cabin," he said without preamble. "Both he and Mr. Bradley refuse to take their sleepers."

Alana turned at that, and I could read my own thought in her face: Lanton and Bradley had to be nuts. "Has Dr. Epstein explained the reasons behind the procedure?" I asked carefully, mindful of both my responsibilities and my limits here.

"Yes, I have," Kate Epstein's clear soprano came. "Dr. Lanton says that his work requires both of them to stay awake through the cascade point."

"Work? What sort of work?"

A pause, and Lanton's voice replaced Kate's. "Captain, this is Dr. Lanton. Rik and I are involved in an experimental type of therapy here. The personal details are confidential, but I assure you that it presents no danger either to us or to you."

Therapy. Great. I could feel anger starting to churn in my gut at Lanton's casual arrogance in neglecting to inform me ahead of time that he had more than transport in mind for my ship. By all rights I should freeze the countdown and sit Lanton down in a corner somewhere until *I* was convinced everything was as safe as he said. But time was money in this business; and if Lanton was glossing things over he could probably do so in finer detail that I could catch him on,

anyway. "Mr. Bradley?" I called. "You agree to pass up your sleeper, as well?"

"Yes, sir," came the mousy voice.

"All right. Dr. Epstein, you and Mr. Leeds can go ahead and finish your rounds."

"Well," Alana said as I flipped off the intercom, "at least if something goes wrong the record will clear us of any fault at the inquest."

"You're a genuine ray of sunshine," I told her sourly. "What else could I have done?"

"Raked Lanton over the coals for some information. We're at least entitled to know what's going on."

"Oh, we'll find out, all right. As soon as we're through the point I'm going to haul Lanton up here for a long, cozy chat." I checked the readouts. Cascade point in seventeen minutes. "Look, you might as well go to your cabin and hit the sack. I know it's your turn, but you were up late with that spare parts delivery and you're due some downtime."

She hesitated; wanting to accept, no doubt, but slowed by considerations of duty. "Well . . . all right. I'm taking the next one, then. I don't know, though; maybe you shouldn't be up here alone. In case Lanton's miscalculated."

"You mean if Bradley goes berserk or something?" That thought had been lurking in my mind, too, though it sounded rather ridiculous when spoken out loud. Still . . . "I can lower the pressure in the passenger deck corridor to half an atmosphere. That'll be enough to lock the doors without triggering any vacuum alarms."

"Leaves Lanton on his own in case of trouble . . . but I suppose that's okay."

"He's the one who's so sure it's safe. Go on, now—get out of here."

She nodded and headed for the door. She paused there, though, her hand resting on the release. "Don't just haul Lanton away from Bradley when you want to talk to him," she called back over her shoulder. "Try to run into him in the lounge or somewhere instead when he's already alone. It might be hard on Bradley to know you two were off somewhere together talking about him." She slapped the release, almost viciously, and was gone.

I stared after her for a long minute, wondering if I'd actually seen a crack in that heavy armor plate. The bleep of the intercom brought me back to the task at hand, Kate telling me the passengers were all down and that she, Leeds, and Wilkinson had taken their own sleepers. One by one the other six crewers also checked in. Within ten minutes they would be asleep, and I would be in sole charge of my ship.

Twelve minutes to go. Even with the *Dancer*'s old manual setup there was little that needed to be done. I laid the hard copy of the computer's instructions where it would be legible but not in the way, shut down all the external sensors and control surfaces, and put the computer and other electronic equipment into neutral/standby mode. The artificial gravity I left on; I'd tried a cascade point without it once and would never do so again. Then I waited, trying not to think of what was coming . . . and at the appropriate time I lifted the safety cover and twisted the field generator control knob.

And suddenly there were five of us in the room.

I will never understand how the first person to test the Colloton Drive ever made it past this point. The images silently surrounding me a bare arm's length away were life-size, lifelike, and—at first glance, anyway—as solid as the panels and chairs they seemed to have displaced. It took a careful look to realize they were actually slightly transparent, like some kind of colored glass, and a little experimentation at that point would show they had less substance than air. They were nothing but ghosts, specters straight out of childhood's scariest stories. Which merely added to the discomfort . . . because all of them were me.

Five seconds later the second set of images appeared, perfectly aligned with the first. After that they came more and more quickly, as the spacing between them similarly decreased, forming an ever-expanding horizontal cross with me at the center. I watched—forced myself to watch—knew I *had* to watch—as the lines continued to lengthen, watched until they were so long that I could no longer discern whether any more were being added.

I took a long, shuddering breath—peripherally aware that the images nearest me were doing the same—and wiped a shaking hand across my forehead. *You don't have to look*, I told myself, eyes rigidly fixed on the back of the image in front of me. *You've seen it all before. What's the point?* But I'd fought this fight before, and I knew in advance I would lose. There was indeed no more point to it than there was to pressing a bruise, but it held an equal degree of compulsion. Bracing myself, I turned my head and gazed down the line of images strung out to my left.

The armchair philosophers may still quibble over what the cascade point images "really" are, but those of us who fly the small ships figured it out long ago. The Colloton field puts us into a different type of space, possibly an entire universe worth of it—that much is established fact. Somehow this space links us into a set of alternate realities, universes that might have been if things had gone differently . . . and what I was therefore seeing around me were images of what I would be doing in each of those universes.

Sure, the theory has problems. Obviously, I should generate a separate pseudoreality every time I choose ham instead of turkey for lunch, and just as obviously such trivial changes don't make it into the pattern. Only the four images closest to me are ever exactly my doubles; even the next ones in line are noticeably if subtly different. But it's not a matter of subconscious suggestion, either. Too many of the images are . . . unexpected . . . for that.

It was no great feat to locate the images I particularly needed to see: the white-and-gold liner captain's uniforms stood out brilliantly among the more dingy jumpsuits and coveralls on either side. Liner captain. In charge of a fully equipped, fully modernized ship; treated with the respect and admiration such a position brought. It could have been—*should* have been. And to make things worse, I knew the precise decision that had lost it to me.

It had been eight years now since the uniforms had appeared among my cascade images; ten since the day I'd thrown Lord Hendrik's son off the bridge of the training ship and simultaneously guaranteed myself a

blackballing with every major company in the business. Could I have handled the situation differently? Probably. Should I have? Given the state of the art then, no. A man who, after three training missions, still went borderline claustrophobic every time he had to stay awake through a cascade point had no business aboard a ship, let alone on its bridge. Hendrik might have forgiven me once he thought things through. The kid, who was forced into a ground position with the firm, never did. Eventually, of course, he took over the business.

I had no way of knowing that four years later the Aker-Ming Autotorque would eliminate the need for *anyone* to stay awake through cascade maneuvers. I doubt seriously the kid appreciated the irony of it all.

In the eight years since the liner captain uniforms had appeared they had been gradually moving away from me along all four arms of the cross. Five more years, I estimated, and they would be far enough down the line to disappear into the mass of images crowded together out there. Whether my reaction to that event would be relief or sadness I didn't yet know, but there was no doubt in my mind that it would in some way be the end of a chapter in my life. I gazed at the figures for another minute . . . and then, with my ritual squeezing of the bruise accomplished, I let my eyes drift up and down the rest of the line.

They were unremarkable, for the most part: minor variations in my appearance or clothing. The handful that had once showed me in some nonspaceing job had long since vanished toward infinity; I'd been out here a long time. Perhaps too long . . . a thought the

half-dozen or so gaps in each arm of the pattern underlined with unnecessary force. I'd told Bradley that ships like the *Dancer* rarely crashed, a perfectly true statement; but what I hadn't mentioned was that the chances of simply disappearing en route were something rather higher. None of us liked to think about that, especially during critical operations like cascade point maneuvers. But the gaps in the image pattern were a continual reminder that people still died in space. In six possible realities, apparently, I'd made a decision that killed me.

Taking another deep breath, I forced all of that as far from my mind as I could and activated the *Dancer*'s flywheel.

Even on the bridge the hum was audible as the massive chunk of metal began to spin. A minute later it had reached its top speed . . . and the entire ship's counterrotation began to register on the gyroscope set behind glass in the ceiling above my head. The device looked out of place, a decided anachronism among the modern instruments, control circuits, and readouts filling the bridge. But using it was the only way a ship our size could find its way safely through a cascade point. The enhanced electron tunneling effect that fouled up electronic instrument performance was well understood; what was still needed was a way to predict the precise effect a given cascade point rotation would generate. Without such predictability, readings couldn't even be given adjustment factors. Cascade navigation thus had to fall back on gross electrical and purely mechanical systems: flywheel, physical gyroscope, simple on-off controls, and a nonelectronic decision maker. Me.

Slowly, the long needle above me crept around its dial. I watched its reflection carefully in the magnifying mirror, a system that allowed me to see the indicator without having to break my neck looking up over my shoulder. Around me, the cascade images did their own slow dance, a strange kaleidoscopic thing that moved the images and gaps around within each branch of the cross, while the branches themselves remained stationary relative to me. The effect was unexplained. Mathematically, the basic idea was relatively straightforward: the space we were in right now could be described by a type of bilinear conformal mapping— specifically, a conjugate inversion that maps lines into circles. From that point it was all downhill, the details tangling into a soup of singularities, branch points, and confluent Riemann surfaces; but what it all eventually boiled down to was that a yaw rotation of the ship here would become a linear translation when I shut down the field generator and we reentered normal space. The *Dancer*'s rotation was coming up in two degrees now, which for the particular configuration we were in meant we were already about half a light-year closer to our destination. Another—I checked the printout—one point three six and I would shut down the flywheel, letting the *Dancer*'s momentum carry her an extra point two degree for a grand total of eight light-years.

The needle crept to the mark, and I threw the flywheel switch, simultaneously giving my full attention over to the gyro. Theoretically, over or undershooting the mark could be corrected during the next cascade point—or by fiddling the flywheel back

and forth now—but it was simpler not to have to correct at all. The need to make sure we were stationary was another matter entirely; if the *Dancer* were still rotating when I threw the field switch we would wind up strung out along a million kilometers or more of space. I thought of the gaps in my cascade image pattern and shivered.

But that was all the closer death was going to get to me, at least this time. The delicately balanced spin lock worked exactly as it was supposed to, freezing the field switch in place until the ship's rotation was as close to zero as made no difference. I shut off the field and watched my duplicates disappear in reverse order, waiting until the last four vanished before confirming the stars were once again visible through the bridge's tiny viewport. I sighed; and fighting the black depression that always seized me at this point, I turned the *Dancer*'s systems back on and set the computer to figuring our exact position. Someday, I thought, I'd be able to afford to buy Aker-Ming Autotorques and never, *never* have to go through this again.

And someday I'd swim the Pacific Ocean, too.

Slumping back in my chair, I waited for the computer to finish its job and allowed the tears to flow.

Crying, for me, has always been the simplest and fastest way of draining off tension, and I've always felt a little sorry for men who weren't able to appreciate its advantages. This time was no exception, and I was feeling almost back to normal by the time the computer produced its location figures. I was still

poring over them twenty minutes later when Alana returned to the bridge. "Another cascade point successfully hurdled, I see," she commented tiredly. "Hurray for our side."

"I thought you were supposed to be taking a real nap, not just a sleeper's worth," I growled at her over my shoulder.

"I woke up and decided to take a walk," she answered, her voice suddenly businesslike. "What's wrong?"

I handed her a printout, pointed to the underlined numbers. "The gyroscope reading says we're theoretically dead on position. The stars say we're short."

"Wumph!" Frowning intently at the paper, she kicked around the other chair and sat down. "Twenty light-days. That's what, twice the expected error for this point? Great. You double-checked everything, of course?"

"Triple-checked. The computer confirmed the gyro reading, and the astrogate program's got positive ident on twenty stars. Margin of error's no greater than ten light-minutes on either of those."

"Yeah." She eyed me over the pages. "Anything funny in the cargo?"

I gestured to the manifest in front of me. "We've got three boxes of technical equipment that include Ming metal," I said. "All three are in the shield. I checked that before we lifted."

"Maybe the shield's sprung a leak," she suggested doubtfully.

"It's supposed to take a hell of a break before the stuff inside can affect cascade point configuration."

"I can go check if you'd like."

"No, don't bother. There's no rush now, and Wilkinson's had more experience with shield boxes. He can take a look when he wakes up. I'd rather you stay here and help me do a complete programming check. Unless you'd like to obey orders and go back to bed."

She smiled faintly. "No, thanks; I'll stay. Um . . . I could even start things alone if you'd like to go to the lounge for a while."

"I'm fine," I growled, irritated by the suggestion.

"I know," she said. "But Lanton was down there alone when I passed by on my way here."

I'd completely forgotten about Lanton and Bradley, and it took a couple of beats for me to catch on. Cross-examining a man in the middle of cascade depression wasn't a terrifically nice thing to do, but I wasn't feeling terrifically nice at the moment. "Start with the astrogate program," I told Alana, getting to my feet. "Give me a shout if you find anything."

Lanton was still alone in the lounge when I arrived. "Doctor," I nodded to him as I sat down in the chair across from his. "How are you feeling?" The question was more for politeness than information; the four empty glasses on the end table beside him and the half-full one in his hand showed how he'd chosen to deal with his depression. I'd learned long ago that crying was easier on the liver.

He managed a weak smile. "Better, Captain; much better. I was starting to think I was the only one left on the ship."

"You're not even the only one awake," I said. "The

other passengers will be wandering in shortly—you people get a higher-dose sleeper than the crew takes."

He shook his head. "Lord, but that was weird. No wonder you want everyone to sleep through it. I can't remember the last time I felt this rotten."

"It'll pass," I assured him. "How did Mr. Bradley take it?"

"Oh, fine. Much better than I did, though he fell apart just as badly when it was over. I gave him a sedative—the coward's way out, but I wasn't up to more demanding therapy at the moment."

So Bradley wasn't going to be walking in on us any time soon. Good. "Speaking of therapy, Doctor, I think you owe me a little more information about what you're doing."

He nodded and took a swallow from his glass. "Beginning, I suppose, with what exactly Rik is suffering from?"

"That would be nice," I said, vaguely surprised at how civil I was being. Somehow, the sight of Lanton huddled miserably with his liquor had taken all the starch out of my fire-and-brimstone mood. Alana was clearly having a bad effect on me.

"Okay. Well, first and foremost, he is *not* in any way dangerous, either to himself or other people. He has no tendencies even remotely suicidal or homicidal. He's simply . . . permanently disoriented, I suppose, is one way to think of it. His personality seems to slide around in strange ways, generating odd fluctuations in behavior and perception."

Explaining psychiatric concepts in layman's terms obviously wasn't Lanton's forte. "You mean he's

schizophrenic? Or paranoid?" I added, remembering our launch-field conversation.

"Yes and no. He shows some of the symptoms of both—along with those of five or six other maladies—but he doesn't demonstrate the proper biochemical syndrome for any known mental disease. He's a fascinating, scientifically annoying anomaly. I've got whole bubble-packs of data on him, taken over the past five years, and I'm convinced I'm teetering on the edge of a breakthrough. But I've already exhausted all the standard ways of probing a patient's subconscious, and I had to come up with something new." He gestured around him. "This is it."

"This is what? A new form of shock therapy?"

"No, no—you're missing the point. I'm studying Rik's cascade images."

I stared at him for a long moment. Then, getting to my feet, I went to the autobar and drew myself a lager. "With all due respect," I said as I sat down again, "I think you're out of your mind. First of all, the images aren't a product of the deep subconscious or whatever; they're reflections of universes that might have been."

"Perhaps. There *is* some argument about that." He held up a hand as I started to object. "But either way, you have to admit that your conscious or unconscious mind *must* have an influence on them. Invariably, the images that appear show the results of *major* decisions or events in one's life; never the plethora of insignificant choices we all make. Whether the subconscious is choosing among actual images or generating them by itself, it *is* involved with them and therefore can be studied through them."

He seemed to settle slightly in his chair, and I got the feeling this wasn't the first time he'd made that speech. "Even if I grant you all that," I said, "which I'm not sure I do, I think you're running an incredibly stupid risk that the cascade point effects will give Bradley a shove right over the edge. They're hard enough on those of us who *haven't* got psychological problems—what am I telling you this for? *You* saw what it was like, damn it. The last thing I want on my ship is someone who's going to need either complete sedation or a restraint couch all the way to Taimyr!"

I stopped short, suddenly aware that my volume had been steadily increasing. "Sorry," I muttered, draining half of my lager. "Like I said, cascade points are hard on all of us."

He frowned. "What do you mean? You were asleep with everyone else, weren't you?"

"Somebody's got to be awake to handle the maneuver," I said.

"But . . . I thought there were autopilots for cascade points now."

"Sure—the Aker-Ming Autotorque. But they cost nearly twenty-two thousand apiece and have to be replaced every hundred cascade points or so. The big liners and freighters can afford luxuries like that; tramp starmers can't."

"I'm sorry—I didn't know." His expression suggested he was also sorry he hadn't investigated the matter more thoroughly before booking aboard the *Dancer*.

I'd seen that look on people before, and I always hated it. "Don't worry; you're perfectly safe. The

manual method's been used for nearly two centuries, and my crew and I know what we're doing."

His mind was obviously still a half kilometer back. "But how can it be that expensive? I mean, Ming metal's an exotic alloy, sure, but it's only selenium with a little bit of rhenium, after all. You can buy psy-test equipment with Ming-metal parts for a fraction of the cost you quoted."

"And we've got an entire box made of the stuff in our number one cargo hold," I countered. "But making a consistent-property rotation gauge is a good deal harder than rolling sheets or whatever. Anyway, you're evading my question. What are you going to do if Bradley can't take the strain?"

He shrugged, but I could see he didn't take the possibility seriously. "If worst comes to worst, I suppose I could let him sleep while I stayed awake to observe his images. They *do* show up even in your sleep, don't they?"

"So I've heard." I didn't add that I'd feel like a voyeur doing something like that. Psychiatrists, accustomed to poking into other people's minds, clearly had different standards than I did.

"Good. Though that would add another variable," he added thoughtfully. "Well . . . I think Rik can handle it. We'll do it conscious as long as we can."

"And what's going to be your clue that he's *not* handling it? The first time he tries to strangle one of his images? Or maybe when he goes catatonic?"

He gave me an irritated look. "Captain, I *am* a psychiatrist. I'm perfectly capable of reading my patient and picking up any signs of trouble before they

become serious. Rik is going to be all right; let's just leave it at that."

I had no intention of leaving it at that; but just then two more of the passengers wandered into the lounge, so I nodded to Lanton and left. We had five days before the next cascade point, and there would be other opportunities in that time to discuss the issue. If necessary, I would manufacture them.

Alana had only negatives for me when I got back to the bridge. "The astrogate's clean," she told me. "I've pulled a hard copy of the program to check, but the odds that a glitch developed that just happened to look reasonable enough to fool the diagnostic are essentially nil." She waved at the long gyroscope needle above us. "Computer further says the vacuum in the gyro chamber stayed hard throughout the maneuver and that there was no malfunction of the mag-bearing fields."

So the gyroscope hadn't been jinxed by friction into giving a false reading. Combined with the results on the astrogate program, that left damn few places to look. "Has Wilkinson checked in?"

"Yes, and I've got him testing the shield for breaks."

"Good. I'll go down and give him a hand. Have you had time to check out our current course?"

"Not in detail, but the settings look all right to me."

"They did to me, too, but if there's any chance the computer's developed problems we can't take anything for granted. I don't want to be in the wrong position when it's time for the next point."

"Yeah. Well, Pascal's due up here in ten minutes. I guess the astrogate deep-check can wait until then. What did you find out from Lanton?"

With an effort I switched gears. "According to him, Bradley's not going to be any trouble. He sounds more neurotic than psychotic, from Lanton's description, at least at the moment. Unfortunately, Lanton's got this great plan to use cascade images as a research tool, and intends to keep Bradley awake through every point between here and Taimyr."

"He *what?* I don't suppose he's bothered to consider what that might do to Bradley's problems?"

"That's what *I* wanted to know. I never did get an acceptable answer." I moved to the bridge door, poked the release. "Don't worry, we'll pound some sense into him before the next point. See you later."

Wilkinson and Sarojis were both in the number one hold when I arrived, Sarojis offering minor assistance and lots of suggestions as Wilkinson crawled over the shimmery metal box that took up the forward third of the narrow space. Looking down at me as I threaded my way between the other boxes cramming the hold, he shook his head. "Nothing wrong here, Cap'n," he said. "The shield's structurally sound; there's no way the Ming metal inside could affect our configuration."

"No chance of hairline cracks?" I asked.

He held up the detector he'd been using. "I'm checking, but nothing that small would do anything."

I nodded acknowledgement and spent a moment frowning at the box. Ming metal had a number of unique properties inside cascade points, properties that made it both a blessing and a curse to those of us who

had to fly with it. Its unique blessing, of course, was that its electrical, magnetic, and thermodynamic properties were affected only by the absolute angle the ship rotated through, and not by any of the hundred or so other variables in a given cascade maneuver. It was this predictability that finally had made it possible for a cascade point autodrive mechanism to be developed. Of more concern to smaller ships like mine, though, was that Ming metal drastically changed a ship's "configuration"—the size, shape, velocity profile, and so on from which the relation between rotation angle and distance traveled on a given maneuver could be computed. Fortunately, the effect was somewhat analgous to air resistance, in that if one piece of Ming metal were completely enclosed in another, only the outer container's shape, size, and mass would affect the configuration. Hence, the shield. But if it hadn't been breached, then the cargo inside it couldn't have fouled us up. . . . "What are the chances," I asked Wilkinson, "that one of these other boxes contains Ming metal?"

"Without listing it on the manifest?" Sarojis piped up indignantly. He was a dark, intense little man who always seemed loudly astonished whenever anyone did anything either unjust or stupid. Most everyone on the *Dancer* OD'd periodically on his chatter and spent every third day or so avoiding him. Alana and Wilkinson were the only exceptions I knew of, and even Alana got tired of him every so often. "They couldn't do that," Sarojis continued before I could respond. "We could sue them into bankruptcy."

"Only if we make it to Taimyr," I said briefly, my eyes on Wilkinson.

"One way to find out," he returned. Dropping lightly off the shield, he replaced his detector in the open tool box lying on the deck and withdrew a wandlike gadget.

It took two hours to run the wand over every crate in the *Dancer*'s three holds, and we came up with precisely nothing. "Maybe one of the passengers brought some aboard," Sarojis suggested.

"You've got to be richer than any of *our* customers to buy cases with Ming-metal buckles." Wilkinson shook his head. "Cap'n, it's got to be a computer fault, or else something in the gyro."

"Um," I said noncommittally. I hadn't yet told them that I'd checked with Alana midway through all the cargo testing and that she and Pascal had found nothing wrong in their deep-checks of both systems. There was no point in worrying them more than necessary.

I returned to the bridge to find Pascal there alone, slouching in the helm chair and gazing at the displays with a dreamy sort of expression on his face. "Where's Alana?" I asked him, dropping into the other chair and eyeing the pile of diagnostic printouts they'd thoughtfully left for me. "Finally gone to bed?"

"She said she was going to stop by the dining room first and have some dinner," Pascal said, the dreamy expression fading somewhat. "Something about meeting the passengers."

I glanced at my watch, realizing with a start that it was indeed dinnertime. "Maybe I'll go on down, too. Any problems here, first?"

He shook his head. "I have a theory about the

cascade point error," he said, lowering his voice conspiratorially. "I'd rather not say what it is, though, until I've had more time to think about it."

"Sure," I said, and left. Pascal fancied himself a great scientific detective and was always coming up with complex and wholly unrealistic theories in areas far outside his field, with predictable results. Still, nothing he'd ever come up with had been actually dangerous, and there was always the chance he would someday hit on something useful. I hoped this would be the day.

The *Dancer*'s compact dining room was surprisingly crowded for so soon after the first cascade point, but a quick scan of the faces showed me why. Only nine of our twelve passengers had made it out of bed after their first experience with sleepers, but their absence was more than made up for by the six crewers who had opted to eat here tonight instead of in the duty mess. The entire off-duty contingent . . . and it wasn't hard to figure out why.

Bradley, seated between Lanton and Tobbar at one of the two tables, was speaking earnestly as I slipped through the door. " . . . less symbolic than it was an attempt to portray the world from a truly alien viewpoint, a viewpoint he would change every few years. Thus *A Midsummer Wedding* has both the slight fish-eye distortion *and* the color shifts you might get from a water-dwelling creature; also the subtleties of posture and expression that such an alien wouldn't understand and might therefore not get right."

"But isn't strange sensory expression one of the basic foundations of art?" That was Tobbar—so glib

on any topic that you were never quite sure whether he actually knew anything about it or not. "Drawing both eyes on one side of the head, putting nudes at otherwise normal picnics—that sort of thing."

"True, but you mustn't confuse weirdness for its own sake with the consistent, scientifically accurate variations Meyerhäus used."

There was no more, but just then Alana caught my eye from her place at the other table and indicated the empty seat next to her. I went over and sat down, losing the train of Bradley's monologue in the process. "Anything?" she whispered to me.

"A very flat zero," I told her.

She nodded once but didn't say anything, and I noticed her gaze drift back to Bradley. "Knows a lot about art, I see," I commented, oddly irritated by her shift in attention.

"You missed his talk on history," she said. "He got quite a discussion going over there—that mathematician, Dr. Chileogu, also seems to be a history buff. First time I've ever seen Tobbar completely frozen out of a discussion. He certainly seems normal enough."

"Tobbar?"

"Bradley."

"Oh." I looked over at Bradley, who was now listening intently to someone holding forth from the other end of his table. *Permanently disoriented*, Lanton had described him. Was he envisioning himself a professor of art or something right now? Or were his delusions that complete? I didn't know; and at the moment I didn't care. "Well, good for him. Now if you'd care to bring your mind back to ship's business, we still have a problem on our hands."

Alana turned back to me, a slight furrow across her forehead. "I'm open to suggestions," she said. "I was under the impression that we were stuck for the moment."

I clenched my jaw tightly over the retort that wanted to come out. We *were* stuck; and until someone else came up with an idea there really wasn't any reason why Alana shouldn't be down relaxing. "Yeah," I growled, getting to my feet. "Well, keep thinking about it."

"Aren't you going to eat?"

"I'll get something later in the duty mess," I said.

I paused at the door and glanced back. Already her attention was back on Bradley. Heading back upstairs to the duty mess, I programmed myself an unimaginative meal that went down like so much wet cardboard. Afterwards, I went back to my cabin and pulled a tape on cascade point theory.

I was still paging through it two hours later when I fell asleep.

I tried several times in the next five days to run into Lanton on his own, but it seemed that every time I saw him Bradley was tagging along like a well-behaved cocker spaniel. Eventually, I was forced to accept Alana's suggestion that she and Tobbar offer Bradley a tour of the ship, giving me a chance to waylay Lanton in the corridor outside his cabin. The psychiatrist seemed preoccupied and a little annoyed at being so accosted, but I didn't let it bother me.

"No, of course there's no progress yet," he said in response to my question. "I also didn't expect any.

The first cascade point observations were my baseline. I'll be asking questions during the next one, and after that I'll start introducing Rik's reactions to them."

He started to slide past me, but I moved to block him. "Treatment? You never said anything about treatment."

"I didn't think I had to. I *am* legally authorized to administer drugs and such, after all."

"Maybe on the ground," I told him stiffly. "But out here the ship's doctor is the final medical authority. You will *not* give Bradley any drugs or electronic treatment without first clearing it with Dr. Epstein." Something tugged at my mind, but I couldn't be bothered with tracking it down. "As a matter fact, I want you to give her a complete list of all the drugs you've brought aboard before the next cascade point. Anything addictive or potentially dangerous is to be turned over to her for storage in the sleeper cabinet. Understand?"

Lanton's expression stuck somewhere between irritated and stunned. "Oh, come on, Captain, be reasonable—practically every medicine in the book can be dangerous if taken in excessive doses." His face seemed to recover, settling into a bland sort of neutral as his voice similarly adjusted to match it. "Why do you object so strongly to what I'm trying to do for Rik?"

"I'd hurry with that list, Doctor—the next point's scheduled for tomorrow. Good day." Spinning on my heel, I turned and stalked away.

I called back Kate Epstein as soon as I reached my cabin and told her about the list Lanton would be

delivering to her. I got the impression that she, too, thought I was overreacting, but she nevertheless agreed to cooperate. I extracted a promise to keep me informed on what Lanton's work involved, then signed off and returned once more to the Colloton theory tapes that had occupied the bulk of my time the past four days.

But despite the urgency I was feeling—we had less than twenty hours to the next cascade point—the words on my reader screen refused to coalesce into anything that made sense. I gritted my teeth and kept at it until I discovered myself reading the same paragraph for the fourth time and still not getting a word of it. Snapping off my reader in disgust, I stretched out on my bed and tried to track down the source of my distraction.

Obviously, my irritation at Lanton was a good fraction of it. Along with the high-handed way he treated the whole business of Bradley, he'd now added the insult of talking to me in a tone of voice that implied I needed his professional services—and for nothing worse than insisting on my rights as captain of the *Dancer*. I wished to hell I'd paid more attention to the passenger manifest before I'd let the two of them aboard. Next time I'd know better.

Still . . . I had to admit that maybe I *had* overreacted a bit. But it wasn't as if I was being short-tempered without reason. I had plenty of reasons to be worried; Lanton's game of cascade image tag and its possible effects on Bradley, the still-unexplained discrepancy in the last point's maneuvers, the changes I was seeing in Alana—

Alana. Up until that moment I hadn't consciously admitted to myself that she was behaving any differently than usual. But I hadn't flown with her for four years without knowing all of her moods and tendencies, and it was abundantly clear to me that she was slowly getting involved with Bradley.

My anger over such an unexpected turn of events was not in any way motivated by jealousy. Alana was her own woman, and any part of her life not directly related to her duties was none of my business. But I knew that, in this case, her involvement was more than likely her old affinity for broken wings, rising like the phoenix—except that the burning would come afterwards instead of beforehand. I didn't want to see Alana go through that again, especially with someone whose presence I felt responsible for. There was, of course, little I could do directly without risking Alana's notice and probable anger; but I could let Lanton know how I felt by continuing to make things as difficult as possible. And I would.

And with that settled, I managed to push it aside and return to my studies. It is, I suppose, revealing that it never occurred to me at the time how inconsistent my conclusion and proposed course of action really were. After all, the faster Lanton cured Bradley, the faster the broken-wing attraction would disappear and—presumably—the easier Alana would be able to extricate herself. Perhaps, even then, I was secretly starting to wonder if her attraction to him was something more than altruistic.

"Two minutes," Alana said crisply from my right, her tone almost but not quite covering the tension I

knew she must be feeling. "Gyro checks out perfectly."

I made a minor adjustment in my mirror, confirmed that the long needle was set dead on Zero. Behind the mirror, the displays stared blankly at me from the control board, their systems having long since been shut down. I looked at the computer's printout, the field generator control cover, my own hands—anything to keep from looking at Alana. Like me, she was unaccustomed to company during a cascade point, and I was determined to give her what little privacy I could.

"One minute," she said. "You sure we made up enough distance for this to be safe?"

"Positive. The only possible trouble could have come from Epsilon Eridani, and we've made up enough lateral distance to put it the requisite six degrees off our path."

"Do you suppose that could have been the trouble last time? Could we have come too close to something—a black dwarf, maybe, that drifted into our corridor?"

I shrugged, eyes on the clock. "Not according to the charts. Ships have been going to Taimyr a long time, you know, and the whole route's been pretty thoroughly checked out. Even black dwarfs have to come *from* somewhere." Gritting my teeth, I flipped the cover off the knob. "Brace yourself; here we go."

Doing a cascade point along invites introspection, memories of times long past, and melancholy. Doing it with someone else adds instant vertigo and claustrophobia to the list. Alana's images and mine still

appeared in the usual horizontal cross shape, but since we weren't seated facing exactly the same direction, they didn't' overlap. The result was a suffocatingly crowded bridge—crowded, to make things worse, with images that were no longer tied to your own emotions, but would twitch and jerk apparently on their own.

For me, the disadvantages far outweighed the single benefit of having someone there to talk to, but in this case I had had little choice. Alana had steadfastly refused to let me take over from her on two points in a row, and I'd been equally insistent on being awake to watch the proceedings. It was a lousy compromise, but I'd known better than to order Alana off the bridge. She had her pride too.

"Activating flywheel."

Alana's voice brought my mind back to business. I checked the printout one last time, then turned my full attention to the gyro needle. A moment later it began its slow creep, and the dual set of cascade images started into their own convoluted dances. Swallowing hard, I gave my stomach stern orders and held on.

It seemed at times to be lasting forever, but finally it was over. The *Dancer* had been rotated, had been brought to a stop, and had successfully made the transition to real space. I slumped in my seat, feeling a mixture of cascade depression and only marginally decreased tension. The astrogate program's verdict, after all, was still to come.

But I was spared the ordeal of waiting with twiddled thumbs for the computer. Alana had barely gotten the ship's systems going again when the intercom bleeped at me. "Bridge," I answered.

"This is Dr. Lanton," the tight response came. "There's something very wrong with the power supply to my cabin—one of my instruments just burned out on me."

"Is it on fire?" I asked sharply, eyes flicking to the status display. Nothing there indicated any problem.

"Oh, no—there was just a little smoke and that's gone now. But the thing's ruined."

"Well, I'm sorry, Doctor," I said, trying to sound like I meant it. "But I can't be responsible for damage to electronics that are left running through a cascade point. Even something as simple as an AC power line can show small voltage fluc—*oh, damn it!*"

Alana jerked at my exclamation. "What—"

"Lanton!" I shouted, already halfway out of my seat. "Stay put and *don't touch anything*. I'm coming down."

His reply was more question than acknowledgment, but I ignored it. "Alana," I called to her, "call Wilkinson and have him meet me at Lanton's cabin—and tell him to bring a Ming-metal detector."

I caught just a glimpse of her suddenly horrified expression before the door slid shut and I went running down the corridor. There was no reason to run, but I did so anyway.

It was there, of course: a nice, neat Ming-metal dual crossover coil, smack in the center of the ruined neural tracer. At least it *had* been neat; now it was stained with a sticky goo that had dripped onto it from the blackened circuit board above. "Make sure none of it melted off onto something else," I told Wilkinson as he carefully removed the coil. "If it has we'll either

have to gut the machine or find a way to squeeze it inside the shield." He nodded and I stepped over to where Lanton was sitting, the white-hot anger inside me completely overriding my usual depression. "What the *hell* did you think you were doing, bringing that damn thing aboard?" I thundered, dimly aware that the freshly sedated Bradley might hear me from the next cabin but not giving a damn.

His voice, when he answered, was low and artificially calm— whether in stunned reaction to my rage or simply a reflexive habit I didn't know. "I'm very sorry, Captain, but I swear I didn't know the tracer had any Ming metal in it."

"Why not? You told me yourself you could buy things with Ming-metal parts." And I'd let that fact sail blithely by me, a blunder on my part that was probably fueling ninety percent of my anger.

"But I never see the manufacturing specs on anything I use," he said. "It all comes through the Institute's receiving department, and all I get are the operating manuals and such." His eyes flicked to his machine as if he were going to object to Wilkinson's manhandling it. "I guess they must have removed any identification tags, as well."

"I guess they must have," I ground out. Wilkinson had the coil out now, and I watched as he laid it aside and picked up the detector wand again. A minute later he shook his head.

"Clean, Cap'n," he told me, picking up the coil again. "I'll take this one to One Hold and put it away."

I nodded and he left. Gesturing to the other gadgets

spread around the room, I asked, "Is this all you've got, or is there more in Bradley's cabin?"

"No, this is it," Lanton assured me.

"What about your stereovision camera? I know some of those have Ming metal in them."

He frowned. "I don't have any cameras. Who told you I did?"

"I—" I frowned in turn. "You said you were studying Bradley's cascade images."

"Yes, but you can't take pictures of them. They don't register on any kind of film."

I opened my mouth, closed it again. I was sure I'd known that once, but after years of watching the images I'd apparently clean forgotten it. They were so lifelike . . . and I was perhaps getting old. "I assumed someone had come up with a technique that worked," I said stiffly, acutely aware that my attempt to save face wasn't fooling either of us. "How *do* you do it, then?"

"I memorize all of it, of course. Psychiatrists have to have good memories, you know, and there are several drugs that can enhance one's basic abilities."

I'd heard of mnemonic drugs. They were safe, extremely effective, and cost a small fortune. "Do you have any of them with you? If so, I'm going to insist they be locked away."

He shook his head. "I was given a six-month treatment at the Institute before we left. That's the main reason we're on your ship, by the way, instead of something specially chartered. Mnemonic drugs play havoc with otherwise reasonable budgets."

He was making a joke, of course, but it was an

exceedingly tasteless one, and the anger that had been draining out of me reversed its flow. No one needed to remind me that the *Dancer* wasn't up to the Cunard line's standards. "My sympathies to your budget," I said briefly. Turning away, I strode to the door.

"Wait a minute," he called after me. "What are my chances of getting that neural tracer fixed?"

I glanced back over my shoulder. "That probably depends on how good you are with a screwdriver and solder gun," I said, and left.

Alana was over her own cascade depression by the time I returned to the bridge. "I was right," I said as I dropped into my seat. "One of the damned black boxes had a Ming-metal coil."

"I know; Wilkinson called from One Hold." She glanced sideways at me. "I hope you didn't chew Lanton out in front of Bradley."

"Why not?"

"Did you?"

"As it happens, no. Lanton sedated him right after the point again. Why does it matter?"

"Well . . ." She seemed embarrassed. "It might . . . upset him to see you angry. You see, he sort of looks up to you—captain of a star ship and all—"

"Captain of a struggling tramp," I corrected her more harshly than was necessary. "Or didn't you bother to tell him that we're the absolute bottom of the line?"

"I told him," she said steadily. "But he doesn't see things that way. Even in five days aboard he's had a glimpse of how demanding this kind of life is. He's

never been able to hold down a good job himself for very long, and that adds to the awe he feels for all of us."

"I can tell he's got a lot to learn about the universe," I snorted. For some reason the conversation was making me nervous, and I hurried to bring it back to safer regions. "Did your concern for Bradley's idealism leave you enough time to run the astrogate?"

She actually blushed, the first time in years I'd seen her do that. "Yes," she said stiffly. "We're about thirty-two light-days short this time."

"Damn." I hammered the edge of the control board once with my clenched fist, and then began punching computer keys.

"I've already checked that," Alana spoke up. "We'll dig pretty deep into our fuel reserve if we try to make it up through normal space."

I nodded, my fingers coming to a halt. My insistence on maintaining a high fuel reserve was one of the last remnants of Lord Hendrik's training that I still held onto, and despite occasional ribbing from other freighter captains I felt it was a safety precaution worth taking. The alternative to using it, though, wasn't especially pleasant. "All right," I sighed. "Let's clear out enough room for the computer to refigure our course profile. If possible, I'd like to tack the extra fifty light-days onto one of the existing points instead of adding a new one."

She nodded and started typing away at her console as I called down to the engine room to alert Matope. It was a semimajor pain, but the *Dancer*'s computer didn't have enough memory space to handle the

horribly complex Colloton calculations we needed while all the standard operations programming was in place. We would need to shift all but the most critical functions to Matope's manual control, replacing the erased programs later from Pascal's set of master tapes.

It took nearly an hour to get the results, but they turned out to be worth the wait. Not only could we make up our shortfall without an extra point, but with the slightly different stellar configuration we faced now it was going to be possible to actually shorten the duration of one of the points further down the line. That was good news from both practical and psychological considerations. Though I've never been able to prove it, I've long believed that the deepest depressions follow the longest points.

I didn't see any more of Lanton that day, though I heard later that he and Bradley had mingled with the passengers as they always did, Lanton behaving as if nothing at all had happened. Though I knew my crew wasn't likely to go around blabbing about Lanton's Ming-metal blunder, I issued an order anyway to keep the whole matter quiet. It wasn't to save Lanton any embarrassment—that much I was certain of—but beyond that my motives became uncomfortably fuzzy. I finally decided I was doing it for Alana, to keep her from having to explain to Bradley what an idiot his therapist was.

The next point, six days later, went flawlessly, and life aboard ship finally settled into the usual deep-space routine. Alana, Pascal, and I each took eight-

hour shifts on the bridge; Matope, Tobbar, and Sarojis did the same back in the engine room; and Kate Epstein, Leeds, and Wilkinson took turns catering to the occasional whims of our passengers. Off duty, most of the crewers also made an effort to spend at least a little time in the passenger lounge, recognizing the need to be friendly in the part of our business that was mainly word of mouth. Since that first night, though, the exaggerated interest in Bradley the Mental Patient had pretty well evaporated, leaving him as just another passenger in nearly everyone's eyes.

The exception, of course, was Alana.

In some ways, watching her during those weeks was roughly akin to watching a baby bird hacking its way out of its shell. Alana's bridge shift followed mine, and I was often more or less forced to hang around for an hour or so listening to her talk about her day. *Forced* is perhaps the wrong word; obviously, no one was nailing me to my chair. And yet, in another sense, I really *did* have no choice. To the best of my knowledge, I was Alana's only real confidant aboard the *Dancer*, and to have refused to listen would have deprived her of her only verbal sounding board. And the more I listened, the more I realized how vital my participation really was . . . because along with the usual rolls, pitches, and yaws of every embryo relationship, this one had an extra complication: Bradley's personality was beginning to change.

Lanton had said he was on the verge of a break-through, but it had never occurred to me that he might be able to begin genuine treatment aboard ship, let alone that any of its effects would show up en route.

But even to me, who saw Bradley for maybe ten minutes at a time three times a week, the changes were obvious. All the conflicting signals in posture and expression that had bothered me so much at our first meeting diminished steadily until they were virtually gone, showing up only on brief occasions. At the same time, his self-confidence began to increase, and a heretofore unnoticed—by me, at least—sense of humor began to manifest itself. The latter effect bothered me, until Alana explained that a proper sense of humor required both a sense of dignity and an ability to take oneself less than seriously, neither of which Bradley had ever had before. I was duly pleased for her at the progress this showed; privately, I sought out Lanton to find out exactly what he was doing to his patient and the possible hazards thereof. The interview was easy to obtain—Bradley was soloing quite a bit these days—but relatively uninformative. Lanton tossed around a lot of stuff about synaptic fixing and duplicate messenger chemistry, but with visions of a Nobel Prize almost visibly orbiting his head he was in no mood to worry about dangerous side effects. He assured me that nothing he was using was in the slightest way experimental, and that I should go back to flying the *Dancer* and let him worry about Bradley. Or words to that effect.

I really *was* happy for Bradley, of course, but the fact remained that his rapid improvement was playing havoc with Alana's feelings. After years away from the wing-mending business she felt herself painfully rusty at it; and as Bradley continued to get better despite that, she began to wonder out loud whether she

was doing any good, and if not, what right she had to continue hanging around him. At first I thought this was just an effort to hide the growth of other feelings from me, but gradually I began to realize that she was as confused as she sounded about what was happening. Never before in her life, I gathered, had romantic feelings come to her without the framework of a broken-wing operation to both build on and help disguise, and with that scaffolding falling apart around her she was either unable or unwilling to admit to herself what was really going on.

I felt pretty rotten having to sit around watching her flounder, but until she was able to recognize for herself what was happening there wasn't much I could do except listen. I wasn't about to offer any suggestions, especially since I didn't believe in love at first sight in the first place. My only consolation was that Bradley and Lanton were riding round trip with us, which meant that Alana wouldn't have to deal with any sort of separation crisis until we were back on Earth. I'd never had much sympathy for people who expected time to solve all their problems for them, but in this case I couldn't think of anything better to do.

And so matters stood as we went through our eighth and final point and emerged barely eight hundred thousand kilometers from the thriving colony world Taimyr . . . and found it deserted.

"Still nothing," Alana said tightly, her voice reflecting both the remnants of cascade depression and the shock of our impossible discovery. "No response to our call; nothing on any frequency I can pick up. I can't even find the comm satellites' lock signal."

I nodded, my eyes on the scope screen as the *Dancer*'s telescope slowly scanned Taimyr's dark side. No lights showed anywhere. Shifting the aim, I began searching for the nine comm and nav satellites that should be circling the planet. "Alana, call up the astrogate again and find out what it's giving as position uncertainty."

"If you're thinking we're in the wrong system, forget it," she said as she tapped keys.

"Just checking all possibilities," I muttered. The satellites, too, were gone. I leaned back in my seat and bit at my lip.

"Yeah. Well, from eighteen positively identified stars we've got an error of no more than half a light-hour." She swiveled to face me and I saw the fear starting to grow behind her eyes. "Pall, what is going *on* here? Two hundred million people can't just disappear without a trace."

I shrugged helplessly. "A nuclear war could do it, I suppose, and might account for the satellites being gone as well. But there's no reason why anyone on Taimyr should *have* any nuclear weapons." Leaning forward again, I activated the helm. "A better view might help. If there's been some kind of war the major cities should now be big craters surrounded by rubble. I'm going to take us in and see what the day side looks like from high orbit."

"Do you think that's safe? I mean—" She hesitated. "Suppose the attack came from outside Taimyr?"

"What, you mean like an invasion?" I shook my head. "Even if there are alien intelligences somewhere who would want to invade us, we stand just as good a

chance of getting away from orbit as we do from here."

"All right," she sighed. "But I'm setting up a cascade point maneuver, just in case. Do you think we should alert everybody yet?"

"Crewers, yes; passengers, no. I don't want any silly questions until I'm ready to answer them."

We took our time approaching Taimyr, but caution turned out to be unnecessary. No ships, human or otherwise, waited in orbit for us; no one hailed or shot at us; and as I turned the telescope planetward I saw no signs of warfare.

Nor did I see any cities, farmland, factories, or vehicles. It was as if Taimyr the colony had never existed.

"It doesn't make any sense," Matope said after I'd explained things over the crew intercom hookup. "How could a whole colony disappear?"

"I've looked up the records we've got on Taimyr," Pascal spoke up. "Some of the tropical vegetation is pretty fierce in the growth department. If everyone down there was killed by a plague or something, it's possible the plants have overgrown everything."

"Except that most of the cities are in temperate regions," I said shortly, "and two are smack in the middle of deserts. I can't find any of those, either."

"Hmm," Pascal said and fell silent, probably already hard at work on a new theory.

"Captain, you don't intend to land, do you?" Sarojis asked. "If launch facilities are gone and not merely covered over we'd be unable to lift again to orbit."

"I'm aware of that, and I have no intention of landing," I assured him. "But something's happened down there, and I'd like to get back to Earth with at least *some* idea of what."

"Maybe nothing's happened to the colony," Wilkinson said slowly. "Maybe something's happened to *us*."

"Such as?"

"Well . . . this may sound strange, but suppose we've somehow gone back in time, back to before the colony was started."

"That's crazy," Sarojis scoffed before I could say anything. "How could we possibly do something like that?"

"Malfunction of the field generator, maybe?" Wilkinson suggested. "There's a lot we don't know about Colloton space."

"It *doesn't* send ships back in—"

"All right, ease up," I told Sarojis. Beside me Alana snorted suddenly and reached for her keyboard. "I agree the idea sounds crazy, but whole cities don't just walk off, either," I continued. "It's not like there's a calendar we can look at out here, either. If we *were* a hundred years in the past, how would we know it?"

"Check the star positions," Matope offered.

"No good; the astrogate program would have noticed if anything was too far out of place. But I expect that still leaves us a possible century or more to rattle around in."

"No, it doesn't." Alana turned back to me with a grimly satisfied look on her face. "I've just taken

signals from three pulsars. Compensating for our distance from Earth gives the proper rates for all three."

"Any comments on that?" I asked, not expecting any. Pulsar signals occasionally break their normal pattern and suddenly increase their pulse frequency, but it was unlikely to have happened in three of the beasts simultaneously; and in the absence of such a glitch the steady decrease in frequency was as good a calendar as we could expect to find.

There was a short pause; then Tobbar spoke up. "Captain, I think maybe it's time to bring the passengers in on this. We can't hide the fact that we're in Taimyr system, so they're bound to figure out sooner or later that something's wrong. And I think they'll be more cooperative if we volunteer the information rather than making them demand it."

"What do we need *their* cooperation for?" Sarojis snorted.

"If you bothered to listen as much as you talked," Tobbar returned, a bit tartly, "you'd know that Chuck Raines is an advanced student in astrophysics and Dr. Chileogu has done a fair amount of work on Colloton field mathematics. I'd say chances are good that we're going to need help from one or both of them before this is all over."

I looked at Alana, raised my eyebrows questioningly. She hesitated, then nodded. "All right," I said. "Matope, you'll stay on duty down there; Alana will be in command here. Everyone else will assemble in the dining room. The meeting will begin in ten minutes."

I waited for their acknowledgments and then flipped off the intercom. "I'd like to be there," Alana said.

"I know," I said, raising my palms helplessly. "But I *have* to be there, and someone's go to keep an eye on things outside."

"Pascal or Sarojis could do it."

True—and under normal circumstances I'd let them. But we're facing an unknown and potentially dangerous situation, and I need someone here whose judgment I trust."

She took a deep breath, exhaled loudly. "Yeah. Well . . . at least let me listen in by intercom, okay?"

"I'd planned to," I nodded. Reaching over, I touched her shoulder. "Don't worry; Bradley can handle the news."

"I know," she said, with a vehemence that told me she wasn't anywhere near that certain.

Sighing, I flipped the PA switch and made the announcement.

They took the news considerably better than I'd expected them to—possibly, I suspected, because the emotional kick hadn't hit them yet.

"But this is absolutely unbelievable, Captain Durriken," Lissa Steadman said when I'd finished. She was a rising young business-administration type who I half-expected to call for a committee to study the problem. "How could a whole colony simply vanish?"

"My question exactly," I told her. "We don't know yet, but we're going to try and find out before we head back to Earth."

"We're just going to leave?" Mr. Eklund asked timidly from the far end of the table. His hand, on top of the table, gripped his wife's tightly, and I belatedly remembered they'd been going to Taimyr to see a daughter who'd emigrated some thirty years earlier. Of all aboard, they had lost the most when the colony vanished.

"I'm sorry," I told him, "but there's no way we could land and take off again, not if we want to make Earth again on the fuel we have left."

Eklund nodded silently. Beside them, Chuck Raines cleared his throat. "Has anybody considered the possibility that *we're* the ones something has happened to? After all, it's the *Aura Dancer*, not Taimyr, that's been dipping in and out of normal space for the last six weeks. Maybe during all that activity something went wrong."

"The floor is open for suggestions," I said.

"Well . . . I presume you've confirmed we *are* in the Taimyr system. Could we be—oh—out of phase or something with the real universe?"

"Highly poetic," Tobbar spoke up from his corner. "But what does *out of phase* physically mean in this case?"

"Something like a parallel universe, or maybe an alternate time line," Raines suggested. "Some replica of our universe where humans never colonized Taimyr. After all, cascade images are supposed to be views of alternate universes, aren't they? Maybe cascade points are somehow where all the possible paths intersect."

"You've been reading too much science fiction," I

told him. "Cascade images are at least partly psychological, and they certainly have no visible substance.
Besides, if you had to trace the proper path through a
hundred universes every time you went through a
cascade point, you'd lose ninety-nine ships out of
every hundred that tried it."

"Actually, Mr. Raines is not being all *that* far out,"
Dr. Chileogu put in quietly. "It's occasionally been
speculated that the branch cuts and Riemann surfaces
that show up in Colloton theory represent distinct
universes. If so, it would be theoretically possible to
cross between them." He smiled slightly. "But it's
extremely unlikely that a responsible captain would
put his ship through the sort of maneuver that would
be necessary to do such a thing."

"What sort of maneuver would it take?" I asked.

"Basically, a large-angle rotation within the cascade
point. Say, eight degrees or more."

I shook my head, feeling relieved and at the same
time vaguely disappointed that a possible lead had
evaporated. "Our largest angle was just under four
point five degrees."

He shrugged. "As I said."

I glanced around the table, wondering what avenue
to try next. But Wilkinson wasn't ready to abandon
this one yet. "I don't understand what the ship's
rotation has to do with it, Dr. Chileogu," he said. "I
thought the farther you rotated, the farther you went in
real space, and that was all."

"Well . . . it would be easier if I could show you
the curves involved. Basically, you're right about the
distance-angle relation as long as you stay below that

eight degrees I mentioned. But above that point there's a discontinuity, similar to what you get in the curve of the ordinary tangent function at ninety degrees; though unlike the tangent the next arm doesn't start at minus infinity." Chileogu glanced around the room, and I could see him revising the level of his explanation downward. "Anyway, the point is that the first arm of the curve—real rotations of zero to eight point six degrees—gives the complete range of translation distance from zero to infinity, and so that's all a star ship ever uses. If the ship rotates *past* that discontinuity, mathematical theory would say it had gone off the edge of the universe and started over again on a different Riemann surface. What that means physically I don't think anyone knows; but as Captain Durriken pointed out, all our real rotations have been well below the discontinuity."

Wilkinson nodded, apparently satisfied; but the term "real rotation" had now set off a warning bell deep in my own mind. It was an expression I hadn't heard—much less thought about—in years, but I vaguely remembered now that it had concealed a seven-liter can of worms. "Doctor, when you speak of a 'real' rotation, you're referring to a mathematical entity, as opposed to an actual, physical one," I said slowly. "Correct?"

He shrugged. "Correct, but with a ship such as this one the two are for all practical purposes identical. The *Aura Dancer* is a long, perfectly symmetrical craft, with both the Colloton-field generator and Ming-metal cargo shield along the center line. It's only when you start working with the fancier liners,

with their towers and blister lounges and all, that you get a serious divergence."

I nodded carefully and looked around the room. Pascal had already gotten it, from the expression on his face; Wilkinson and Tobbar were starting to. "Could an extra piece of Ming metal, placed several meters off the ship's center line, cause such a divergence?" I asked Chileogu.

"Possibly." He frowned. "Very possibly."

I shifted my gaze to Lanton. His face had gone white. "I think," I said, "I've located the problem."

Seated at the main terminal in Pascal's cramped computer room, Chileogu turned the Ming-metal coil over in his hands and shook his head. "I'm sorry, Captain, but it simply can't be done. A dual crossover winding is one of the most complex shapes in existence, and there's no way I can calculate its effect with a computer this small."

I glanced over his head at Pascal and Lanton, the latter having tagged along after I cut short the meeting and hustled the mathematician down here. "Can't you even get us an estimate?" I asked.

"Certainly. But the estimate could be anywhere up to a factor of three off, which would be worse than useless to you."

I nodded, pursing my lips tightly. "Well, then, how about going on from here? With that coil back in the shield, the real and physical rotations coincide again. Is there some way we can get back to our universe; say, by taking a long step out from Taimyr and two short ones back?"

Chileogu pondered that one for a long minutes. "I would say that it depends on how many universes we're actually dealing with," he said at last. "If there are just two—ours and this one—then rotating past any one discontinuity should do it. But if there are more than two, you'd wind up just going one deeper into the stack if you crossed the wrong line."

"Ouch," Pascal murmured. "And if there are an infinite number, I presume, we'd never get back out?"

The mathematician shrugged uncomfortably. "Very likely."

"But don't the mathematics show how many universes there are?" Lanton spoke up.

"They show how many Riemann surfaces there are," Chileogu corrected. "But physical reality is never obliged to correspond with our theories and constructs. Experimental checks are always required, and to the best of my knowledge no one has ever tried this one."

I thought of all the ships that had simply disappeared, and shivered slightly. "In other words, trying to find the Taimyr colony is out. All right, then. What about the principle of reversibility? Will that let us go back the way we came?"

"Back to Earth?" Chileogu hesitated. "Ye-e-s, I think that would apply here. But to go back don't you need to know . . . ?"

"The real rotations we used to get here," I nodded heavily. "Yeah." We looked at each other, and I saw that he, too, recognized the implications of that requirement.

Lanton, though, was still light-years behind us.

"You act like there's still a problem," he said, looking back and forth between us. "Don't you have records of the rotations we made at each point?"

I was suddenly tired of the psychiatrist. "Pascal, would you explain things to Dr. Lanton—on your way back to the passenger area?"

"Sure." Pascal stepped to Lanton's side and took his arm. "This way, Doctor."

"But—" Lanton's protests were cut off by the closing door.

I sat down carefully on a corner of the console, staring back at the Korusyn 630 that took up most of the room's space. "I take it," Chileogu said quietly, "that you can't get the return-trip parameters?"

"We can get all but the last two points we'd need," I told him. "The ship's basic configuration was normal for all of those, and the Korusyn there can handle them." I shook my head. "But even for those the parameters will be totally different—a two-degree rotation one way might become a one or three on the return trip. It depends on our relation to the galactic magnetic field and angular momentum vectors, closest-approach distance to large masses, and a half-dozen other parameters. Even if we *had* a mathematical expression for the influence Lanton's damn coil had on our first two points, I wouldn't know how to reprogram the machine to take that into account."

Chileogu was silent for a moment. Then, straightening up in his seat, he flexed his fingers. "Well, I suppose we have to start somewhere. Can you clear me a section of memory?"

"Easily. What are you going to do?"

He picked up the coil again. "I can't do a complete calculation, but there are several approximation methods that occasionally work pretty well; they're scattered throughout my technical tapes if your library doesn't have a list. If they give widely varying results—as they probably will, I'm afraid—then we're back where we started. But if they happen to show a close agreement, we can probably use the result with reasonable confidence." He smiled slightly. "*Then* we get to worry about programming it in."

"Yeah. Well, first things first. Alana, have you been listening in?"

"Yes," her voice came promptly through the intercom. "I'm clearing the computer now."

Chileogu left a moment later to fetch his tapes. Pascal returned while he was gone, and I filled him in on what we were going to try. Together, he and Alana had the computer ready by the time Chileogu returned. I considered staying to watch, but common sense told me I would just be in the way, so instead I went up to the bridge and relieved Alana. It wasn't really my shift, but I didn't feel like mixing with the passengers, and I could think and brood as well on the bridge as I could in my cabin. Besides, I had a feeling Alana would like to check up on Bradley.

I'd been sitting there staring at Taimyr for about an hour when the intercom bleeped. "Captain," Alana's voice said, "Can you come down to the dining room right away? Dr. Lanton's come up with an idea I think you'll want to hear."

I resisted my reflexive urge to tell her what Lanton could do with his ideas; her use of my title meant she

wasn't alone. "All right," I sighed. "I'll get Sarojis to take over here and be down in a few minutes."

"I think Dr. Chileogu and Pascal should be here, too."

Something frosty went skittering down my back. Alana knew the importance of what those two were doing. Whatever Lanton's brainstorm was, she must genuinely think it worth listening to. "All right. We'll be there shortly."

They were all waiting quietly around one of the tables when I arrived. Bradley, not surprisingly, was there too, seated next to Alana and across from Lanton. Only the six of us were present; the other passengers, I guessed, were keeping the autobar in the lounge busy. "Okay, let's have it," I said without preamble as I sat down.

"Yes, sir," Lanton said, throwing a quick glance in Pascal's direction. "If I understood Mr. Pascal's earlier explanation correctly, we're basically stuck because there's no way to calibrate the *Aura Dancer*'s instruments to take the, uh, extra Ming metal into account."

"Close enough," I grunted. "So?"

"So, it occurred to me that this 'real' rotation you were talking about ought to have some external manifestations, the same way a gyro needle shows the ship's physical rotation."

"You mean like something outside the viewports?" I frowned.

"No; something inside. I'm referring to the cascade images."

I opened my mouth, closed it again. My first

thought was that it was the world's dumbest idea, but my second was *why not?* "You're saying, what, that the image-shuffling that occurs while we rotate is tied to the real rotation, each shift being a hundredth of a radian or something?"

"Right"—he nodded—"although I don't know whether that kind of calibration would be possible."

I looked at Chileogu. "Doctor?"

The mathematician brought his gaze back from infinity. "I'm not sure what to say. The basic idea is actually not new—Colloton himself showed such a manifestation ought to be present, and several others have suggested the cascade images were it. But I've never heard of any actual test being made of the hypothesis; and from what I've heard of the images, I suspect there are grave practical problems besides. The pattern doesn't change in any mathematically predictable way, so I don't know how you would keep track of the shifts."

"I wouldn't have to," Lanton said. "I've been observing Rik's cascade images throughout the trip. I remember what the pattern looked like at both the beginning and ending of each rotation."

I looked at Bradley, suddenly understanding. His eyes met mine and he nodded fractionally.

"The only problem," Lanton continued, "is that I'm not sure we could set up at either end to do the reverse rotation."

"Chances are good we can," I said absently, my eyes still on Bradley. His expression was strangely hard for someone who was supposedly seeing the way out of permanent exile. Alana, if possible, looked

even less happy. "All rotations are supposed to begin at zero, and since we always go 'forward' we always rotate the same direction."

I glanced back at Lanton to see his eyes go flat, as if he were watching a private movie. "You're right; it *is* the same starting pattern each time. I hadn't really noticed that before, with the changes and all."

"It should be easy enough to check, Captain," Pascal spoke up. "We can compute the physical rotations for the first six points we'll be going through. The real rotations should be the same as on the outbound leg, though, so if Dr. Lanton's right the images will wind up in the same pattern they did before."

"But how—?" Chileogu broke off suddenly. "Ah. You've had a mnemonic treatment?"

Lanton nodded and then looked at me. "I think Mr. Pascal's idea is a good one, Captain, and I don't see any purpose in hanging around here any longer than necessary. Whenever you want to start back—"

"I have a few questions to ask first," I interrupted mildly. I glanced at Bradley, decided to tackle the easier ones first. "Dr. Chileogu, what's the status of your project?"

"The approximations? We've just finished programming the first one; it'll take another hour or so to collect enough data for a plot. I agree with Dr. Lanton, though—we can do the calculations between cascade points as easily as we can do them in orbit here."

"Thank you. Dr. Lanton, you mentioned something about *changes* a minute ago. What exactly did you mean?"

Lanton's eyes flicked to Bradley for an instant. "Well . . . as I told you several weeks ago, a person's mind has a certain effect on the cascade image pattern. Some of the medicines Rik's been taking have slightly altered the—oh, I guess you could call it the *texture* of the pattern."

"Altered it how much?"

"In some cases, fairly extensively." He hesitated, just a bit too long. "But nothing I've done is absolutely irreversible. I should be able to re-create the original conditions before each cascade point."

Deliberately, I leaned back in my chair. "All right. Now let's hear what the problem is."

"I beg your pardon?"

"You heard me." I waved at Bradley and Alana. "Your patient and my first officer look like they're about to leave for a funeral. I want to know why."

Lanton's cheek twitched. "I don't think this is the time or the place to discuss—"

"The problem, Captain," Bradley interrupted quietly, "is that the reversing of the treatments may turn out to be permanent."

It took a moment for that to sink in. When it did I turned my eyes back to Lanton. "Explain."

The psychiatrist took a deep breath. "The day after the second point I used ultrasound to perform a type of minor neurosurgery called synapse fixing. It applies heat to selected regions of the brain to correct a tendency of the nerves to misfire. The effects *can* be reversed . . . but the procedure's been done only rarely, and usually involves unavoidable peripheral damage."

I felt my gaze hardening into an icy stare. "In other words," I bit out, "not only will the progress he's made lately be reversed, but he'll likely wind up worse off than he started. Is that it?"

Lanton squirmed uncomfortably, avoiding my eyes. "I don't *know* that he will. Now that I've found a treatment— "

"You're about to give him a brand-new disorder," I snapped. *"Damn* it all, Lanton, you are the most cold-blooded—"

"Captain."

Bradley's single word cut off my flow of invective faster than anything but hard vacuum could have. "What?" I said.

"Captain, I understand how you feel." His voice was quiet but firm; and though the tightness remained in his expression, it had been joined by an odd sort of determination. "But Dr. Lanton wasn't really trying to maneuver you into supporting something unethical. For the record, I've already agreed to work with him on this; I'll put that on tape if you'd like." He smiled slightly. "And before you bring it up, I *am* recognized as legally responsible for my actions, so as long as Dr. Lanton and I agree on a course of treatment your agreement is not required."

"That's not entirely true," I ground out. "As a ship's captain in deep space, I have full legal power here. If I say he can't do something to you, he can't. Period."

Bradley's face never changed. "Perhaps. But unless you can find another way to get us back to Earth, I don't see that you have any other choice."

I stared into those eyes for a couple of heartbeats. Then, slowly, my gaze swept the table, touching in turn all the others as they sat watching me, awaiting my decision. The thought of deliberately sending Bradley back to his permanent disorientation—*really* permanent, this time—left a taste in my mouth that was practically gagging in its intensity. But Bradley was right . . . and at the moment I didn't have any better ideas.

"Pascal," I said, "you and Dr. Chileogu will first of all get some output on that program of yours. Alana, as soon as they're finished you'll take the computer back and calculate the parameters for our first point. *You* two"—I glared in turn at Bradley and Lanton— "will be ready to test this image theory of yours. You'll do the observations in your cabin as usual, and tell me afterwards whether we duplicated the rotation exactly or came out short or long. Questions? All right; dismissed."

After all, I thought amid the general scraping of chairs, *for the first six points all Bradley will need to do is cut back on medicines. That means twenty-eight days or so before any irreversible surgery is done.*

I had just that long to come up with another answer.

We left orbit three hours later, pushing outward on low drive to conserve fuel. That plus the course I'd chosen meant another ten hours until we were in position for the first point, but none of that time was wasted. Pascal and Chileogu were able to program and run two more approximation schemes; the results, unfortunately, were not encouraging. Any two of the

three plots had a fair chance of agreeing over ranges of half a degree or so, but there was no consistency at all over the larger angles we would need to use. Chileogu refused to throw in the towel, pointing out that he had another six methods to try and making vague noises about statistical curve-fitting schemes. I promised him all the computer time he needed between point maneuvers, but privately I conceded defeat. Lanton's method now seemed our only chance . . . if it worked.

I handled the first point myself, double-checking all parameters beforehand and taking special pains to run the gyro needle as close to the proper angle as I could. As with any such hand operation, of course, perfection was not quite possible, and I ran the *Dancer* something under a hundredth of a degree long. I'm not sure what I was expecting from this first test, but I *was* more than a little surprised when Lanton accurately reported that we'd slightly overshot the mark.

"It looks like it'll work," Alana commented from her cabin when I relayed the news. She didn't sound too enthusiastic.

"Maybe," I said, feeling somehow the need to be as skeptical as possible. "We'll see what happens when he starts taking Bradley off the drugs. I find it hard to believe that the man's mental state can be played like a yo-yo, and if it can't be we'll have to go with whatever statistical magic Chileogu can put together."

Alana gave a little snort that she'd probably meant to be a laugh. "Hard to know which way to hope, isn't it?"

Yeah." I hesitated for a second, running the duty

arrangements over in my mind. "Look, why don't you take the next few days off, at least until the next point. Sarojis can take your shift up here."

"That's all right," she sighed. "I—if it's all the same with you, I'd rather save any offtime until later. Rik will . . . need my help more then."

"Okay," I told her. "Just let me know when you want it and the time's yours."

We continued on our slow way, and with each cascade point I became more and more convinced that Lanton really would be able to guide us through those last two critical points. His accuracy for the first four maneuvers was a solid hundred percent, and on the fifth maneuver we got to within point zero two percent of the computer's previous reading by deliberately jockeying the *Dancer* back and forth until Bradley's image pattern was exactly as Lanton remembered it. After that even Matope was willing to be cautiously optimistic; and if it hadn't been for one small cloud hanging over my head I probably would have been as happy as the rest of the passengers had become.

The cloud, of course, being Bradley.

I'd been wrong about how much his improvement had been due to the drugs Lanton had been giving him, and every time I saw him that ill-considered line about playing his mind like a yo-yo came back to haunt me. Slowly, but very steadily, Bradley was regressing toward his original mental state. His face went first, his expressions beginning to crowd each other again as if he were unable to decide which of several moods should be expressed at any given moment. His eyes took on that shining, nervous look I hated so much;

just occasionally at first, but gradually becoming more and more frequent, until it seemed to be almost his norm. And yet, even though he certainly saw what was happening to him, not once did I hear him say anything that could be taken as resentment or complaint. It was as if the chance to save twenty other lives was so important to him that it was worth any sacrifice. I thought occasionally about Alana's comment that he'd never before had a sense of dignity, and wondered if he would lose it again to his illness. But I didn't wonder about it all that much; I was too busy worrying about Alana.

I hadn't expected her to take Bradley's regression well, of course—to someone with Alana's wing-mending instincts a backsliding patient would be both insult *and* injury. What I wasn't prepared for was her abrupt withdrawal into a shell of silence on the issue which no amount of gentle probing could crack open. I tried to be patient with her, figuring that eventually the need to talk would overcome her reticence; but as the day for what Lanton described as "minor surgery" approached, I finally decided I couldn't wait any longer. On the day after our sixth cascade point, I quit being subtle and forced the issue.

"Whatever I'm feeling, it isn't any concern of yours," she said, her fingers playing across the bridge controls as she prepared to take over from me. Her hands belied the calmness in her voice: I knew her usual checkout routine as well as my own, and she lost the sequence no fewer than three times while I watched.

"I think it is," I told her. "Aside from questions of

friendship, you're a member of my crew, and anything that might interfere with your efficiency is my concern."

She snorted. "I've been under worse strains than this without falling apart."

"I know. But you've never buried yourself this deeply before, and it worries me."

"I know. I'm . . . sorry. If I could put it into words— " She shrugged helplessly.

"Are you worried about Bradley?" I prompted. "Don't forget that, whatever Lanton has to do here, he'll have all the resources of the Swedish Psychiatric Institute available to undo it."

"I know. But . . . he's going to come out of it a different person. Even Lanton has to admit that."

"Well . . . maybe it'll wind up being a change for the better."

It was a stupid remark, and her scornful look didn't make me feel any better about having made it. "Oh, come *on*. Have you *ever* heard of an injury that did any real good? Because that's what it's going to be—an injury."

And suddenly I understood. "You're afraid you won't like him afterwards, aren't you? At least not the way you do now?"

"Why should that be so unreasonable?" she snapped. "I'm a damn fussy person, you know—I don't like an awful lot of people. I can't afford to . . . to lose any of them." She turned her back on me abruptly, and I saw her shoulders shake once.

I waited a decent interval before speaking. "Look, Alana, you're not in any shape to stay up here alone.

Why don't you go down to your cabin and pull yourself together, and then go and spend some time with Bradley."

"I'm all right," she mumbled. "I can take my shift."

"I know. But . . . at the moment I imagine Rik needs you more than I do. Go on, get below."

She resisted for a few more minutes, but eventually I bent her sense of duty far enough and she left. For a long time afterwards I just sat and stared at the stars, my thoughts whistling around my head in tight orbit. What *would* the effect of the new Bradley be on Alana? She'd been right—whatever happened, it wasn't likely to be an improvement. If her interest was really only in wing-mending, Lanton's work would provide her with a brand-new challenge. But I didn't think even Alana was able to fool herself like that anymore. She cared about him, for sure, and if he changed too much that feeling might well die.

And I wouldn't lose her when we landed.

I thought about it long and hard, examining it and the rest of our situation from several angles. Finally, I leaned forward and keyed the intercom. Wilkinson was off duty in his cabin; from the time it took him to answer he must have been asleep as well. "Wilkinson, you got a good look at the damage in Lanton's neural whatsis machine. How hard would it be to fix?"

"Uh . . . well, that's hard to say. The thing that spit goop all over the Ming-metal coil was a standard voltage regulator board—we're bound to have spares aboard. But there may be other damage, too. I'd have to run an analyzer over it to find out if anything else is

dead. Whether we would have replacements is another question."

"Okay. Starting right now, you're relieved of all other duty until you've got that thing running again. Use anything you need from ship's spares—" I hesitated—"and you can even pirate from our cargo if necessary."

"Yes, sir." He was wide awake now. "I gather there's a deadline?"

"Lanton's going to be doing some ultrasound work on Bradley in fifty-eight hours. You need to be done before that. Oh, and you'll need to work in Lanton's cabin—I don't want the machine moved at all."

"Got it. If you'll clear it with Lanton, I can be up there in twenty minutes."

Lanton wasn't all that enthusiastic about letting Wilkinson set up shop in his cabin, especially when I wouldn't explain my reasons to him, but eventually he gave in. I alerted Kate Epstein that she would have to do without Wilkinson for a while, and then called Matope to confirm the project's access to tools and spares.

And then, for the time being, it was all over but the waiting. I resumed my examination of the viewport, wondering if I were being smart or just pipe-dreaming.

Two days later—barely eight hours before Bradley's operation was due to begin—Wilkinson finally reported that the neural tracer was once again operational.

"This better be important," Lanton fumed as he took his place at the dining-room table. "I'm already behind schedule in my equipment setup as it is."

I glanced around at the others before replying. Pascal and Chileogu, fresh from their latest attempt at making sense from their assortment of plots, seemed tired and irritated by this interruption. Bradley and Alana, holding hands tightly under the table, looked more resigned than anything else. Everyone seemed a little gaunt, but that was probably my imagination— certainly we weren't on anything approaching starvation rations yet. "Actually, Doctor," I said, looking back at Lanton, "you're not in nearly the hurry you think. There's not going to be any operation."

That got everyone's full attention. "You've found another way?" Alana breathed, a hint of life touching her eyes for the first time in days.

"I think so. Dr. Chileogu, I need to know first whether a current running through Ming metal would change its effect on the ship's rotation."

He frowned, then shrugged. "Probably. I have no idea how, though."

A good thing I'd had the gadget fixed, then. "Doesn't matter. Dr. Lanton, can you tell me approximately when in the cascade point your neural tracer burned out?"

"I can tell you exactly. It was just as the images started disappearing, right at the end."

I nodded; I'd hoped it was either the turning on or off of the field generator that had done it. That would make the logistics a whole lot easier. "Good. Then we'll all set. What we're going to do, you see, is reenact that particular maneuver."

"What good will *that* do?" Lanton asked, his tone more puzzled than belligerent.

"It should get us home." I waved toward the outer hull. "For the past two days we've been moving toward a position where the galactic field and other parameters are almost exactly the same as we had when we went through that point—providing your neural tracer is one and we're heading back toward Taimyr. In another two days we'll turn around and get our velocity vector lined up correctly. Then, with your tracer running, we're going to fire up the generator and rotate the same amount—by gyro reading—as we did then. *You*"—I leveled a finger at Lanton— "will be on the bridge during that operation, and you will note the exact configuration of your cascade images at that moment. Then, *without shutting off the generator,* we'll rotate *back* to zero; zero as defined by your cascade pattern, since it may be different from gyro zero. At that time, I'll take the Ming metal from your tracer, walk it to the number one hold, and stuff it into the cargo shield; and we'll rotate the ship again until we reach your memorized cascade pattern. Since the physical and real rotations are identical in that configuration, that'll give us the real angle we rotated through the last time—"

"And from *that* we can figure the angle we'll need to make going the other direction!" Alana all but shouted.

I nodded. "Once we've rotated back to zero to regain our starting point, of course." I looked around at them again. Lanton and Bradley still seemed confused, though the latter was starting to catch Alana's enthusiasm. Chileogu was scribbling on a notepad, and Pascal just sat there with his mouth

slightly open. Probably astonished that he hadn't come up with such a crazy idea himself. "That's all I have to say," I told them. "If you have any comments later—"

"I have one, Captain."

I looked at Bradley in some surprise. "Yes?"

He swallowed visibly. "It seems to me, sir, that what you're going to need is a set of cascade images that vary a lot, so that the pattern you're looking for is a distinctive one. I don't think Dr. Lanton's are suitable for that."

"I see." Of course, while Lanton had been studying Bradley's images, Bradley couldn't help but see his, as well. "Lanton? How about it?"

The psychiatrist shrugged. "I admit they're a little bland—I haven't had a very exciting life. But they'll do."

"I doubt it." Bradley looked back at me. "Captain, I'd like to volunteer."

"You don't know what you're saying," I told him. "Each rotation will take twice as long as the ones you've already been through. *And* there'll be two of them back to back; *and* the field won't be shut down between them, because I want to know if the images drift while I'm moving the coil around the ship. Multiply by about five what you've felt afterwards and you'll get some idea what it'll be like." I shook my head. "I'm grateful for your offer, but I can't let more people than necessary go through that."

"I appreciate that. But I'm still going to do it."

We locked eyes for a long moment . . . and the word *dignity* flashed through my mind. "In that case,

I accept," I said. "Other questions? Thank you for stopping by."

They got the message and began standing up . . . all except Alana. Bradley whispered something to her, but she shook her head and whispered back. Reluctantly, he let go of her hand and followed the others out of the room.

"Question?" I asked Alana when we were alone, bracing for an argument over the role I was letting Bradley take.

"You're right about the extra stress staying in Colloton space that long will create," she said. "That probably goes double for anyone running around in it. I'd expect a lot more vertigo, for starters, and that could make movement dangerous."

"Would you rather Bradley had his brain scorched?"

She flinched, but stood her ground. "My objection isn't with the method—it's with who's going to be bouncing off the *Dancer*'s walls."

"Oh. Well, before you get the idea you're being left out of things, let me point out that *you're* going to be handling bridge duties for the maneuver."

"Fine; but since I'm going to be up anyway I want the job of running the Ming metal back and forth instead."

I shook my head. "No. You're right about the unknowns involved with this, which is why *I'm* going to do it."

"I'm five years younger than you are," she said, ticking off fingers. "I also have a higher stress index, better balance, and I'm in better physical condition."

She hesitated. "And I'm not haunted by white uniforms in my cascade images," she added gently.

Coming from anyone else, that last would have been like a knife in the gut. But from Alana, it somehow didn't even sting. "The assignments are nonnegotiable," I said, getting to my feet. "Now if you'll excuse me, I have to catch a little sleep before my next shift."

She didn't respond. When I left she was still sitting there, staring through the shiny surface of the table.

"Here we go. Good Luck," were the last words I heard Alana say before the intercom was shut down and I was alone in Lanton's cabin. Alone, but not for long; a moment later my first doubles appeared. Raising my wrist, I keyed my chrono to stopwatch mode and waited, ears tingling with the faint ululation of the Colloton field generator. The sound, inaudible from the bridge, reminded me of my trainee days, before the *Dancer* . . . before Lord Hendrik and his fool-headed kid. . . . Shaking my head sharply, I focused on the images, waiting for them to begin their one-dimensional allemande.

They did, and I started my timer. With the lines to the bridge dead I was going to have to rely on the image movements to let me know when the first part of the maneuver was over; moving the ming metal around the ship while we were at the wrong end of our rotation or—worse—while we were still moving would probably end our chances of getting back for good. Mindful of the pranks cascade points could play on a person's time sense, I'd had Pascal calculate the approximate times each rotation would take. Depend-

ing on how accurate they turned out to be, they might simply let me limit how soon I started worrying.

It wasn't a pleasant wait. On the bridge, I had various duties to perform; here, I didn't have even that much distraction from the ghosts surrounding me. Sitting next to the humming neural tracer, I watched the images flicker in and out, white uniforms dos-adosing with the coveralls and the gaps.

Ghosts. *Haunted*. I'd never seriously thought of them like that before, but now I found I couldn't see them in any other way. I imagined I could see knowing smiles on the liner captains' faces, or feel a coldness from the gaps where I'd died. Pure autosuggestion, of course . . . and yet, it forced me for probably the first time to consider what exactly the images were doing to me.

They were making me chronically discontented with my life.

My first reaction to such an idea was to immediately justify my resentment. I'd been cheated out of the chance to be a success in my field; trapped at the bottom of the heap by idiots who ranked political weaselcraft higher than flying skill. I had a *right* to feel dumped on.

And yet . . .

My watch clicked at me: the first rotation should be about over. I reset it and waited, watching the images. With agonizing slowness they came to a stop . . . and then started moving again in what I could per-suade myself was the opposite direction. I started my watch again and let my eyes defocus a bit. The next time the dance stopped, it would be time to move

Lanton's damn coil to the hold and bring my ship back to normal.

My ship. I listened to the way the words echoed around my brain. *My ship.* No liner captain owned his own ship. He was an employee, like any other in the company; forever under the basilisk eye of those selfsame idiots who'd fired me once for doing my job. The space junk being sparser and all that aside, would I *really* have been happier in a job like that? Would I have enjoyed being caught between management on one hand and upper-crusty passengers on the other? Enjoyed, hell—would I have *survived* it? For the first time in ten years I began to wonder if perhaps Lord Hendrik had known what he was doing when he booted me out of his company.

Deliberately, I searched out the white uniforms far off to my left and watched as they popped in and out of different slots in the long line. Perhaps that was why there were so few of them, I thought suddenly; perhaps, even while I was pretending otherwise, I'd been smart enough to make decisions that had kept me out of the running for that particular treadmill. The picture that created made me smile: my subconscious chasing around with secret memos, hiding basic policy matters from my righteously indignant conscious mind.

The click of my watch made me jump. Taking a deep breath, I picked up a screwdriver from the tool pouch laid out beside the neural tracer and gave my full attention to the images. Slow . . . slower . . . stopped. I waited a full two minutes to make sure, then flipped off the tracer and got to work.

I'd had plenty of practice in the past two days, but

it still took me nearly five minutes to extricate the coil from the maze of equipment surrounding it. That was no particular problem— we'd allowed seven minutes for the disassembly—but I was still starting to sweat as I got to my feet and headed for the door.

And promptly fell on my face.

Alana's reference to enhanced vertigo apart, I hadn't expected anything that strong quite so soon. Swallowing hard, I tried to ignore the feeling of lying on a steep hill and crawled toward the nearest wall. Using it as a support, I got to my feet, waited for the cabin to stop spinning, and shuffled over to the door. Fortunately, all the doors between me and One Hold had been locked open, so I didn't have to worry about getting to the release. Still shuffling, I maneuvered through the opening and started down the corridor, moving as quickly as I could. The trip—fifteen meters of corridor, and squeezing through One Hold's cargo to get to the shield—normally took less than three minutes. We'd allowed ten; but already I could see that was going to be tight. I kept my eyes on the wall beside me and concentrated on moving my feet . . . which was probably why I was nearly to the stairway before I noticed the kaleidoscope dance my cascade images were doing.

While the ship was at rest.

I stopped short, the pattern shifts ceasing as I did so. The thing I feared most about this whole trick was happening: moving the Ming metal was changing our real angle in Colloton space.

I don't know how long I leaned there with the sweat trickling down my forehead, but it was probably no more than a minute before I forced myself to get

moving again. There were now exactly two responses Alana could make: go on to the endpoint Lanton had just memorized, or try and compensate somehow for the shift I was causing. The former course felt intuitively wrong, but the latter might well be impossible to do—and neither had any particular mathematical backing that Chileogu had been able to find. For me, the worst part of it was the fact that I was now completely out of the decision process. No matter how fast I got the coil locked away, there was no way I was going to make it back up two flights of stairs to the bridge. Like everyone else on board, I was just going to have to trust Alana's judgment.

I slammed into the edge of the stairway opening, nearly starting my downward trip headfirst before I got a grip on the railing. The coil, jarred from my sweaty hand, went on ahead of me, clanging like a muffled bell as it bounced to the deck below. I followed a good deal more slowly, the writhing images around me adding to my vertigo. By now, the rest of my body was also starting to react to the stress, and I had to stop every few steps as a wave of nausea or fatigue washed over me. It seemed forever before I finally reached the bottom of the stairs. The coil had rolled to the middle of the corridor; retrieving it on hands and knees, I got back to the wall and hauled myself to my feet. I didn't dare look at my watch.

The cargo hold was the worst part yet. The floor was swaying freely by then, like an ocean vessel in heavy seas, and through the reddish haze surrounding me, the stacks of boxes I staggered between seemed ready to hurl themselves down upon my head. I don't remember how many times I shied back from what

appeared to be a breaking wave of crates, only to slam into the stack behind me. Finally, though, I made it to the open area in front of the shield door. I was halfway across the gap, moving again on hands and knees, when my watch sounded the one-minute warning. With a desperate lunge, I pushed myself up and forward, running full tilt into the Ming-metal wall. More from good luck than anything else, my free hand caught the handle; and as I fell backwards the door swung open. For a moment I hung there, trying to get my trembling muscles to respond. Then, slowly, I got my feet under me and stood up. Reaching through the opening, I let go of the coil and watched it drop into the gap between two boxes. The hold was swaying more and more violently now; timing my move carefully, I shoved on the handle and collapsed to the deck. The door slammed shut with a thunderclap that tried to take the top of my head with it. I hung on just long enough to see that the door was indeed closed, and then gave in to the darkness.

I'm told they found me sleeping with my back against the shield door, making sure it couldn't accidentally come open.

I was lying on my back when I came to, and the first thing I saw when I opened my eyes was Kate Epstein's face. "How do you feel?" she asked.

"Fine," I told her, frowning as I glanced around. This wasn't my cabin. . . . With a start I recognized the humming in my ear. "What the hell am I doing in Lanton's cabin?" I growled.

Kate shrugged and reached over my shoulder, shutting off the neural tracer. "We needed Dr. Lan-

ton's neural equipment, and the tracer wasn't supposed to be moved. A variant of the mountain/Mohammed problem, I guess you could say."

I grunted. "How'd the point maneuver go? Was Alana able to figure out a correction factor?"

"It went perfectly well," Alana's voice came from my right. I turned my head, to find her sitting next to the door. "I think we're out of the woods now, Pall—that four-point-four physical rotation turned out to be more like nine point one once the coil was out of the way. If Chileogu's right about reversibility applying here, we should be back in our own universe now. I guess we won't know for sure until we go through the next point and reach Earth."

"Is that nine point one with or without a correction factor?" I asked, my stomach tightening in anticipation. We might not be out of the woods quite yet.

"No correction needed," she said. "The images on the bridge stayed rock-steady the whole time."

"But . . . *I* saw them shifting."

"Yes, you told us that. Our best guess—excuse me; *Pascal*'s best guess—is that you were getting that because you were moving relative to the field generator, that if you'd made a complete loop around it you would've come back to the original cascade pattern again. Chileogu's trying to prove that mathematically, but I doubt he'll be able to until he gets to better facilities."

"Uh-huh." Something wasn't quite right here. "You say I *told* you about the images? When?"

Alana hesitated, looked at Kate. "Actually, Captain," the doctor said gently, "you've been conscious quite a bit during the past four days. The reason

you don't remember any of it is that the connection
between your short-term and long-term memories got
a little scrambled—probably another effect of your
jaunt across all those field lines. It looks like that
part's healed itself, though, so you shouldn't have nay
more memory problems."

"Oh, great. What sort of problems *will* I have more
of?"

"Nothing major. You might have balance difficul-
ties for a while, and you'll likely have a mild migraine
or two within the next couple of weeks. But indica-
tions are that all of it is very temporary."

I looked back at Alana. "Four days. We'll need to
set up our last calibration run soon."

"All taken care of," she assured me. "We're turning
around later today to get our velocity vector pointing
back toward Taimyr again, and we'll be able to do the
run tomorrow."

"Who's going to handle it?"

"Who do you think?" she snorted. "Rik, Lanton,
and me, with maybe some help from Pascal."

I'd known that answer was coming, but it still made
my mouth go dry. "No way," I told her, struggling to
sit up. "You aren't going to go through this hell. I can
manage—"

"Ease up, Pall," Alana interrupted me. "Weren't
you paying attention? The real angle doesn't drift
when the Ming metal is moved, and that means we can
shut down the field generator while I'm taking the coil
from here to One Hold again."

I sank back onto the bed, feeling foolish. "Oh.
Right."

Getting to her feet, Alana came over to me and

patted my shoulder. "Don't worry," she said in a kinder tone. "We've got things under control. You've done the hard part; just relax and let us do the rest."

"Okay," I agreed, trying to hide my misgivings.

It was just as well that I did. Thirty-eight hours later Alana used our last gram of fuel in a flawless bit of flying that put us into a deep Earth orbit. The patrol boats that had responded to her emergency signal were waiting there, loaded with the fuel we would need to land.

Six hours after that, we were home.

They checked me into a hospital, just to be on the safe side, and the next four days were filled with a flurry of tests, medical interviews, and bumpy wheelchair rides. Surprisingly—to me, anyway—I was also nailed by two media types who wanted the more traditional type of interview. Apparently, the *Dancer*'s trip to elsewhere and back was getting a fair amount of publicity. Just how widespread the coverage was, though, I didn't realize until my last day there, when an official-looking CompNote was delivered to my room.

It was from Lord Hendrik.

I snapped the sealer and unfolded the paper. The first couple of paragraphs—the greetings, congratulations on my safe return, and such—I skipped over quickly, my eyes zeroing in on the business portion of the letter.

As you may or may not know, I have recently come out of semiretirement to serve on the Board of Directors of TranStar Enterprises, headquartered here in

Nairobi. With excellent contacts both in Africa and in the so-called Black Colony chain, our passenger load is expanding rapidly, and we are constantly on the search of experienced and resourceful pilots we can entrust them to. The news reports of your recent close call brought you to my mind again after all these years, and I thought you might be interested in discussing—

A knock on the door interrupted my reading. "Come in," I called, looking up.

It was Alana. "Hi, Pall, how are you doing?" she asked, walking over to the bed and giving me a brief once-over. In one hand she carried a slender plastic portfolio.

"Bored silly," I told her. "I think I'm about ready to check out—they've finished all the standard tests without finding anything, and I'm tired of lying around while they dream up new ones."

"What a shame," she said with mock sorrow. "And after I brought you all this reading material, too." She hefted the portfolio.

"What is it, your resignation?" I asked, trying to keep my voice light. There was no point making this any more painful for either of us than necessary.

But she just frowned. "Don't be silly. It's a whole batch of new contracts I've picked up for us in the past few days. Some really good ones, too, from name corporations. I think people are starting to see what a really good carrier we are."

I snorted. "Aside from the thirty-six or whatever penalty clauses we invoked on this trip?"

"Oh, that's all in here too. The Swedish Institute's

not even going to put up a fight—they're paying off everything, including your hospital bills and the patrol's rescue fee. Probably figured Lanton's glitch was going to make them look bad enough without them trying to chisel us out of damages too." She hesitated, and an odd expression flickered across her face. "Were you really expecting me to jump ship?"

"I was about eighty percent sure," I said, fudging my estimate down about nineteen points. "After all, this is where Rik Bradley's going to be, and you . . . rather like him. Don't you?"

She shrugged. "I don't know *what* I feel for him, to be perfectly honest. I like him, sure—like him a lot. But my life's out there"—she gestured skyward— "and I don't think I can give that up for anyone. At least, not for him."

"You could take a leave of absence," I told her, feeling like a prize fool but determined to give her every possible option. "Maybe once you spend some real time on a planet, you'd find you like it."

"And maybe I wouldn't," she countered. "And when I decided I'd had enough, where would the *Dancer* be? Probably nowhere I'd ever be able to get to you." She looked me straight in the eye and all traces of levity vanished from her voice. "Like I told you once before, Pall, I can't afford to lose *any* of my friends."

I took a deep breath and carefully let it out. "Well. I guess that's all settled. Good. Now, if you'll be kind enough to tell the nurse out by the monitor station that I'm signing out, I'll get dressed and we'll get back to the ship."

"Great. It'll be good to have you back." Smiling, she disappeared out into the corridor.

Carefully, I got my clothes out of the closet and began putting them on, an odd mixture of victory and defeat settling into my stomach. Alana was staying with the *Dancer*, which was certainly what I'd wanted . . . and yet, I couldn't help but feel that in some ways her decision was more a default than a real, active choice. Was she coming back because she wanted to, or merely because we were a safer course than the set of unknowns that Bradley offered? If the latter, it was clear that her old burns weren't entirely healed; that she still had a ways—maybe a long ways—to go. But that was all right. I may not have the talent she did for healing bruised souls, but if time and distance were what she needed, the *Dancer* and I could supply her with both.

I was just sealing my boots when Alana returned. "Finished? Good. They're getting your release ready, so let's go. Don't forget your letter," she added, pointing at Lord Hendrik's CompNote.

"This? It's nothing," I told her, crumpling it up and tossing it toward the wastebasket. "Just some junk mail from an old admirer."

Six months later, on our third point out from Prima, a new image of myself in liner captain's white appeared in my cascade pattern. I looked at it long and hard . . . and then did something I'd never done before for such an image.

I wished it lots of luck.